A THING CALLED LOVE

JILL SANDERS

GRAYTON

This is a work of fiction. Names, characters, places, and incidents either are the product of the author's imagination or are used fictitiously, and any resemblance to actual persons, living or dead, business establishments, events, or locales is entirely coincidental.

A THING CALLED LOVE

DIGITAL ISBN: 978-1-945100-21-5

PRINT ISBN: 9798672025759

Text copyright © 2021 Grayton Press

All rights reserved.

Copyeditor: Erica Ellis – inkdeepediting.com

SUMMARY

Kara has put everything on the line to make other people's wedding dreams come true. Watching all the happy couples is truly the best job ever. Yet somehow her luck in men resulted in her only dating jerks. What does a woman have to do to find the man of her dreams? Drown?

Coming from the insanely successful Jordan clan, Conner has always struggled with knowing what he wanted to do in life. But after rescuing the sexy newcomer, suddenly he knows exactly what he wants in his future.

To Erica Ellis

Thank you for being the best editor an
author could ask for.

Here's to the next 70 books!

PROLOGUE

Conner stood back and watched his cousin Suzie walk down the flower-lined aisle. Out of all of his family members who had gotten married, somehow seeing Suzie as a bride hit him the hardest.

Even when Riley, his little sister, had gotten married two years back, it hadn't affected him this much. Sure, he'd been proud. After all, he liked Carter Miller, the man who had married her. Who wouldn't? The guy was great.

But the fact that Suzie was marrying Aiden Brogan, one of Conner's best friends since... well, birth, made him even prouder. Maybe that's why this wedding hit him so hard? That his little cousin could find love with someone she'd known her entire life made him wonder if he'd missed out himself. Could he have overlooked the one? Was he missing out on his chance?

After all, this was his fourth cousin to marry in the past four years. They were dropping like flies. Or so everyone at the wedding was saying.

Of course, that left big targets on the remaining Jordan cousins. There were only three Jordan men left unmarried

—Conner's little brother Jacob, their cousin George, and himself. The three of them were the last of the available bachelors in the Jordan clan.

Whatever the reason for his new feelings, he was slowly realizing that he was tired of not knowing the direction he was going. He'd struggled with it his entire life, really.

Sure, he'd attended school and had actually been good at it without even really trying. He'd flown through two years of college, then had returned to Pride when he'd grown bored of classes. Since then, he'd been doing odd jobs. Sometimes he worked for his cousin Sara's husband Parker, helping him at his construction company. Other times, he helped out at the family's restaurant, the Golden Oar. Hell, one time he'd even modeled for one of his mother's paintings. Not that anyone could tell, since she'd positioned him far off in the distance in one of her oil paintings of the beach.

Still, he'd found plenty to keep him from getting bored. Then, over a year ago, he had started training as a reservist at the Coast Guard facility just outside of town. How he'd let Allen Masters talk him into it was a mystery. He'd run into the guy at the Golden Oar one evening. The man was eating dinner with his family and had started up a conversation.

The following day, he'd showed up at Conner's door bright and early. He'd officially signed up to join and had undergone the rigorous application process.

He wasn't even quite sure that's what he wanted out of life. Still, he'd allowed Allen to drag him down to the facility each day and, well, that had been thirteen months ago. Passing the eight-week boot camp had been easy enough. Conner thrived on the challenging physical training. Maybe that's why he'd stuck it out. If only he could get behind it as much as his family members got behind their careers.

Being dedicated to something bigger was what Conner really wanted at this point.

Watching Suzie and Aiden dance under the spotlight and look at one another with such... admiration, he realized for the first time in his life that he was lonely.

Pride, Oregon, being the small town that it was, didn't have a revolving door of women to date like he'd had at college. Since his return, he'd found plenty of friends to hang out with and even an ex or two to play with. But nothing that had given him the opportunity to move beyond a few nights of fun. If that's really what he was looking for.

CHAPTER ONE

Kara Jenkins had pulled off another perfect wedding. Watching all of the guests stroll slowly out of the massive barn she and her older sister, Robin, had turned into their venue, Sunset Weddings, she took a deep breath of the fall Oregon air and smiled.

"We did it again," Robin said, coming up beside her.

"Yes." She tried not to squeal with excitement. "We did." She always felt pumped after such an event. She knew she should be tired after spending more than twenty hours on her feet, but somehow, she was raring to go still.

"I'm going to make sure the cleaning crew gets started," Robin said and, after running her hand down Kara's arm, she turned away.

"I'll..." She turned to go help, but Robin glanced back at her.

"No, you've done enough for today. You started three hours earlier than I did. Go, relax." She motioned to the big doors.

Off in the distance, she could see the lights from their

little cottage, which they had purchased together more than a year ago, when they had moved to Pride.

"I mean it." Robin gave her the look, the kind Kara knew all too well, which meant her older sister wouldn't stop nagging her if she tried to help out.

"Fine." She sighed. "I'm going to go take a walk on the beach." She nodded to the warm dark night outside the large barn doors.

"Enjoy," Robin threw over her shoulder as she moved off to oversee the cleaning up.

Smiling, Kara stepped out into the warm night. There were still a handful of guests standing around in the gravel parking lot, talking. She made her way past the large covered patio, littered with tables and chairs. The entire area was lit up by bright Edison string lights, which hung from the beams and tree branches overhead. She toed off her sandaled heels and carried them with her after she stepped onto the soft sand.

Strolling along the Oregon coast with a full moon lighting her way and the warm fall breeze heating her up, she could just imagine her fairytale dreams for her future life coming true.

This is why she'd talked Robin into going into business with her shortly after their grandfather had passed away, leaving them each a large chunk of inheritance.

Robin had been away at college, studying business, while Kara had a freshly printed high school diploma in her hands and no idea what she wanted to do in life.

Ever since she'd been a child, she'd scoured through wedding magazines. It was one of her favorite pastimes. When she'd been old enough to start dating and realized that men were nothing like the fairytales she'd grown up with, it somehow became an addiction.

She'd lose herself in all things weddings. Which is where she'd gotten the idea to open Sunset Weddings. Convincing her sister to pool their inheritance together hadn't taken as long as she'd thought it would.

When she'd shown Robin the property she'd found on the coast of Oregon, in the small town they both knew was where their parents had fallen in love, Robin had surprised her by agreeing.

She couldn't count the times she'd passed by the large red barn as a child and dreamed of holding her own wedding in the massive building. She'd lucked out when she'd looked and found it up for sale.

It had taken several months of renovations to turn the massive barn into the beautiful venue it was today. But, thanks to Parker Clark, the renovations had gone smoothly.

The first year of their business had gone off without a hitch. They were making more money than they had expected, and the word was out that Sunset Weddings was the hottest wedding venue along the Oregon coast.

They had it all. The redesigned interior was sleek and chic. They'd added an enormous stone fireplace along the back wall with a wide hearth, which made for a great backdrop for wedding pictures. The two-story barn had been turned into an elegant piece of art, with the enormous antique chandelier that Blake Jordan had found for them at an estate sale. Actually, it was all thanks to Blake that the interior was as classy as it was. The woman knew how to find items that enhanced the rustic and elegant atmosphere.

It was all Kara could have dreamed and hoped for. She loved her work. Loved every aspect of it. Well, okay, if she was being honest, she didn't understand any of the actual business side, but that's where Robin came in. Robin had always been great with numbers and planning.

Setting her shoes down in the sand, she sat and listened to the surf, pulling her knees to her chest. Growing up in the city, she'd dreamed about living near the ocean. Dreamed of being in a small town that welcomed her and her own dreams. Pride, so far, filled that position perfectly.

Of course, she'd known it would. She'd grown up hearing her parents talk about the magical Christmas they'd been snowed in and had fallen in love here and had known it was the place she wanted to be.

Even now, her parents continued to come back to Pride once a year for their anniversary.

She remembered spending summers in Pride with her family. Each time they'd returned, she'd fallen more in love with the area.

Her mind turned to a different kind of love. One that she'd struggled with her entire life.

Why was it that she had a knack for dating jerks? It seemed the more she dated, the more they came out of the woodwork. It started with her very first boyfriend, Leo. Leo had been one of the most popular boys in middle school. When he'd asked Kara to dance, she'd melted inside.

She'd been the envy of every girl in her class when they'd officially started dating the following week. It hadn't taken long to realize that Leo was a jerk. When she'd caught him kissing Lori, a girl a grade above Kara, he'd tried to explain it away, saying that Lori had come on to him. Kara hadn't bought it and had moved on to date Tom, another popular boy and one of Leo's friends.

Two weeks after they'd made it official, Tom had broken things off with her when he'd attended a party and hooked up with Lori. Lori again! That had caused the two friends to fall out. It was funny—they hadn't fought over both of them dating Kara, but cheating on her with Lori had set the friends in a downward spiral.

She wondered why she wasn't a girl that boys fought over. What did Lori have that she didn't? Okay, so her boobs had come in a lot earlier than Kara's had, but still, they were both B cups.

She'd avoided dating again until high school. Joe hadn't been popular or in sports. He'd been a quiet, shy boy she'd had a crush on for almost a year before asking him to a dance.

It had taken him another year to show his true colors. The first time he pushed her, she'd thought it was an accident or that she'd somehow caused his anger. But when he'd up and slapped her after a school dance, she'd walked away for good.

The next week, Joe had started a rumor that she'd cheated on him and he'd broken things off.

Since she no longer cared about what he thought, she hadn't fought the rumor. Her friends knew her too well to fall for his lies. Besides, she'd had the bruised cheek to prove her point with her closest friends.

It was a year later before she opened herself up to another man. Matt was her first real love. She'd run into him at a coffee house one weekend her junior year. He didn't go to her school and, in fact, hadn't even finished high school. He worked at an auto parts store and lived above someone's garage.

She'd fallen hard for him. He'd been kind, caring, and funny. He played the guitar, which she'd found totally sexy. She'd been shocked when, one day, he'd informed her that he had signed up for the army and was shipping out for bootcamp the following day.

He'd admitted that he didn't love her as much as she

loved him, that he'd never felt as strongly about her as she had about him.

That was almost two years ago, and she still struggled with opening her heart again. Maybe she wasn't destined to find love. Maybe she was only destined to help others with their joyous days.

No. She closed her eyes and shook her head. That couldn't be what her life was all about.

Standing up suddenly, she felt the heat of the night and felt a need to cool off. She pulled her dress over her head, tossed it in the sand, and headed for the surf in nothing but her matching bra and panties.

The cool water on her feet felt wonderful. She told herself that she'd stop if she got too deep or she became too chilled. After all, she'd seen way too many movies and knew better than to go swimming in the ocean after dark.

Walking to where the water was up to her knees, she let the cold Pacific saltwater wash over her completely.

It felt as if she could cleanse herself from her past, from her bad decisions. If only she could break her string of bad luck when it came to men.

She started floating in the surf, assured that she was only in knee-deep water, as she watched the moon above her and dodged the waves lapping and tossing her around.

Should she join one of those dating apps her friends were talking about? After all, she knew the chances of meeting someone in a small town were slim. After living in Pride for a year, she practically knew everyone in town already.

Sure, there were a few with potential. But none she'd felt any sort of... *pow* with.

Of course, the Jordan clan had a plethora of fine men. She'd met all of them, including the three unmarried men around her own age. The most eligible bachelors along the Oregon coast, as everyone in town was calling them.

She'd found them all extremely sexy. Lilly's brother George was nice, but a total player. Every time she'd seen him, he'd had a different woman on his arm.

Riley's twin brother, Jacob, was sweet, almost too sweet. He was very helpful at every event their family went to, including the wedding tonight.

Riley's older brother Conner was, well, the sexiest man she'd seen by far. But he'd only said a few words to her in the entire time Kara had been in town.

"Where's the beer?" had been the first, followed by, "Where's your sister?"

That had given her the idea that Robin had somehow caught his eye, which in the sister code book meant he was off the menu.

A large wave almost knocked her under, causing her to realize that she'd drifted out farther than she'd wanted. When she tried to stand up, her feet found only water underneath.

Sputtering slightly, she spit out the saltwater she'd sucked into her mouth and glanced towards land. Another larger wave pushed her head under again. This time she coughed as she spat out the water.

When another wave hit her, she began to understand that she was in major trouble.

Suddenly, strong arms circled her waist, pulling her up to the surface. She sucked in a large breath of air and held onto the muscles holding her.

She let her body go lax when he started working hard to get them both to safety.

When she felt the sand under her feet once again, she began laughing. She didn't know why she did so, other than she was happy she was back to safety. Happy that she'd been saved.

"Are you okay?" a deep voice said as they rolled onto the sand. Water pushed sand into her bra and under her panties, but she didn't care. She was safe.

Her fingers dug into the coldness of the sand, and she enjoyed the coarseness of the grains under her fingertips.

Instead of answering, she continued to laugh.

"Hey." Strong arms grabbed her shoulders. "Are you okay?" he repeated.

The moonlight hit his dark wet hair, and for a moment his slate blue eyes almost glowed in the darkness. She knew instantly that it was Conner. But for a moment, it was as if she was seeing the man for the first time.

"Yes," she finally answered him, "I'm okay."

CHAPTER TWO

Conner was hovering over Kara, looking down into her hazel eyes and trying to decide if she needed further saving.

The fact that she was still smiling threw him off, and he frowned down at her.

Her dark hair was fanned out on the wet sand, and her pale skin almost glowed in the moonlight. The sight of her beauty at such a time caused him to wonder if she was part mermaid. After all, most women he'd known didn't look half as good as she did after almost drowning.

He'd noticed how pretty she was the first time he'd seen her, but she'd been busy and, well, he'd been trying to avoid entanglements. The kind that came with sexy hazel eyes and skin he wanted to spend a lifetime exploring. He balled his hands beside her head in the sand to try and control the urge to lean down and kiss her lips, which were turned upward in a slight grin.

"You didn't hit your head or anything, did you?" he asked, suddenly concerned that she was concussed.

"No." He watched her lips as she smiled up at him. "I'm fine."

Why hadn't he seen how beautiful she was before? Sure, he'd noticed her. But the woman laughing back up at him now was a complete knockout. He felt the effects of her smile deep down in his soul.

Then he realized what had happened to her, how reckless she'd been, and he felt his temper grow.

"Do you have any idea how stupid it is to swim in the ocean at night?" he heard himself saying.

The fact that he too had been on an evening swim when he'd bumped into her warm body fighting the tide did little to discourage him from berating her.

His words cause that sexy smile to slip from her lips, and he realized he should have kept his mouth shut.

"I wasn't in any danger. Not really," she said softly. He knew instantly that she didn't believe her own words. Then she reached up and shoved his shoulder until he moved to sit next to her in the sand.

"Really? Because it sure seemed like that to me." He'd grown up around his sister and cousins and knew all too well that women always won arguments. He shouldn't have tried to argue with her, but he wanted to stress how badly things could have turned out if he hadn't been there.

Her eyes ran over him and narrowed. "What were you doing out here?" she finally asked him. Her eyes landed on his bare chest and then dashed down quickly to his boxer briefs.

"I'm highly trained at swimming in the ocean. I grew up here," he replied quickly.

There was a moment of quiet, then she started laughing again.

"You're Kara, right?" he asked, trying to test her, just in case she really had bumped her head.

He knew for a fact that there were sharp rocks under

the surf. When he'd been around ten, he'd found out about them himself after being pulled under the surf one summer and needing stitches in his shoulder. The scares he'd gotten were a constant reminder to him of how dangerous the ocean could be.

"You're Conner, right?" she said back to him as she hugged her knees to her chest.

He leaned back in the sand and watched her. Her wet hair hung over her shoulders now, and he could see that her makeup had washed away with the saltwater. Her clear face made her even more beautiful.

"Yeah." He glanced back towards the brightly lit barn. "Shouldn't you be in there... doing whatever it is you do after weddings?"

"I'm all done for the night." She glanced over at him. "You didn't answer my question."

"I was training," he said quickly. "You don't have to help clean up or... whatever?"

She smiled again. "No. Training for what?"

He frowned and glanced off towards the dark waters. "A test." He knew he was being vague but didn't really feel like going into the details at the moment. "You shouldn't swim after dark. If you're not a strong swimmer, you shouldn't be in the ocean at all."

He watched her change. Gone was the laughter, replaced by annoyance. Good. He wanted to make sure his point got through to her clearly.

"I'm a strong swimmer." She started dusting herself off and made a move to stand.

He jumped up and took her elbow to help pull her up. When her body bumped against his, he felt a zip of desire race through him like lightning. It knocked the breath out of him, forcing him to freeze up. Well, everything except for his dick, which tented his still wet boxer briefs.

"Why are you training at night?" she asked. If she'd noticed his reaction to her, she thankfully didn't mention it.

Then she glanced down at his hand, still holding her arm. He would have let go, but he was still trying to figure out what to do with the knowledge that no one else had ever caused his body to react quite like this so quickly before. Well, at least since he'd gotten out of the awkward puberty stage.

"I train at all hours. Any free time I can get." He needed to find a way to get himself under control. He glanced off down the dark beach. "You live in The Roger family's old cottage."

She glanced in the direction of the place and nodded. "Yeah, we got the barn when we purchased the cottage." She glanced back down the beach at the barn.

"Did you buy the home for the barn or vice versa?" he asked, curious what had brought the sisters to Pride.

"The cottage was a bonus." She glanced back over at him. "You're in the Coast Guard, aren't you?"

He shrugged. "For now." He glanced back out over the dark water and thought about his future. The one that was still so uncertain to him. "Why weddings?"

She smiled and shrugged slightly. "It's been my dream for as long as I can remember," she answered with a slight sigh.

He frowned as she talked about starting the business with her sister. He'd finally distracted her from asking him questions about himself. He didn't mind listening to her talk about her life, but just knowing that all she thought about was perfect weddings reminded him that he'd never believed he was the marrying type.

Sure, the rest of the Jordan clan had been ripe for marriage. But not Conner. For as long as he could remember, he'd known that he would never marry. Never have a family and be... normal.

He wasn't made for it. There was just something inside him that told him he'd go through life lonely.

It wasn't as if he was torturing himself, it's just... he was different. He didn't have what it took to be normal. Things like knowing what he wanted out of life. Knowing which direction that he wanted to take. Hell, he couldn't even make up his mind what color socks to put on most mornings. Which is why signing up with the Coast Guard Reserve had been perfect. Those choices had been taken from him.

Every other Jordan had their own missions in life. They had all known what they wanted or who they wanted to be. Starting with his parents.

Iian Jordan was one of the best chefs along the Oregon coast. He'd taken over the family restaurant at a young age after losing his hearing in a boat accident that had taken the life of his father, Conner's grandfather George.

Conner's mother, Allison, was an artist anyone who knew anything about art knew of. His mother's paintings hung in some of the most prestigious art galleries around the world. He had even heard that there was one hanging in the White House somewhere.

Riley, his younger sister, and their cousin Lilly had opened up a boutique, Classy and Sassy, in town a few years back. The store was a huge success.

Riley's twin, Jacob, had gone to engineering school and had just taken on the job of overseeing construction of their uncle Todd's latest crazy scheme, Hidden Cove, a subdivision on the massive land Todd had purchased to keep the crooked developer Thomas Carson from getting his hands on the land.

Of course, everyone in town knew of the deal and how the man had been supposedly tied to an illegal gambling and fighting ring that had been dispersed off the coast by his new cousin-in-law, Aiden. Aiden had recently been voted in as sheriff of Pride after his father retired due to injuries caused by a goon supposedly hired by Carson to hide the gambling ring.

Hell, even Conner's little brother had a more important job than he did. Sure, saving lives was no walk in the park. In the past year he'd been more disciplined than he had his entire life, both physically and mentally. Still, lots of others had come and gone in the training facility with abilities just like his own, which made him feel more like a cog than a leader.

The same could be said for each of his cousins. Everyone in the Jordan clan had their path in life plotted out already.

"I lost you," Kara said, touching his bare shoulder, getting his attention again. "I always seem to lose people when I start chatting about my job." She sighed. "It's not like all I think about is weddings," she said with a half-smile. "Honest. I'm not one of those crazed women who hear wedding bells every time I meet a man." She chuckled. "Honest." She held up her fingers in a scout's promise.

"That's the Boy Scout promise." His eyes ran over her slowly. "I doubt they would have let you in their little group. Especially looking like that."

For the first time since he'd pulled her out of the water, she seemed to realize what she was wearing and crossed her arms over her chest as she glanced around the dark beach.

"I... left my dress..." She did a full circle. "Somewhere."

He chuckled as she started frantically looking for her clothes.

"You were probably closer to the barn when you entered the water," he pointed out. "We're well past your cottage now."

She gasped when she realized where they were. "I guess I must have been in the water longer than I thought."

"I'll walk with you. My things are that way as well." He started walking down the beach, not waiting for her. She easily caught up with him, dropping her hands from shielding the view of her sexy body from him.

He quickly glanced over and smiled at the sexy view before continuing to walk back down the beach.

"You know, I saw that," she said, falling in step with him.

"Hey, I'm just as naked as you are," he reminded her.

"Right," she said, and he could hear the laughter in her tone.

"Besides, what you're wearing could easily be a swimsuit instead of..." He stopped and looked down at her. He noticed she didn't lift her arms to cover her body this time. Instead, she stood there, facing him with her chin in the air as she smiled at him. "Instead of a matching set of lacy underwear," he finished. He leaned closer and squinted. "Are those blue?"

"Purple," she answered quickly. "My favorite color."

He stopped and quickly picked up his clothes and dusted off the dinner jacket that he'd worn to the wedding earlier.

"You just dumped your suit in the sand?" She almost gasped.

He chuckled. "No, I set it over the log carefully," he corrected as he shook out his shirt and dress pants, then folded them all and carried his shoes and clothing, figuring he'd pull them on when he was a little drier. "What did you do with your dress? Hang it up?" He glanced down the dark beach as if to prove his point.

"No, I..." She sighed in frustration. "Whatever." She shook her head in defeat and started marching down the beach again.

He caught up with her as he held in a chuckle. He could tell she was growing more agitated at him since she was sprinting down the beach at this point. When she almost passed her dress and shoes sitting in the sand, the laughter slipped out. She turned and glared at him, which only made him laugh even harder.

CHAPTER THREE

Kara was so over Conner hanging around at this point. Sure, he was nice to look at in the moonlight. The way the moonbeams bounced off his perfect pecs and six-pack had her mouth watering.

In the last few moments, however, she could tell he was laughing at her and she was growing tired of being told she was irresponsible.

She bent down and picked up her dress and shoes, then suddenly stopped when she realized she'd just berated him for setting his suit carefully on a large piece of driftwood. If there had been any driftwood in sight, she would have hung her dress over it, but instead, she'd just tossed it in the sand earlier.

She'd been so focused on needing to cool off and clear her mind that she hadn't thought about her own clothes.

Turning back to him, she sighed.

"I'm sorry, I must be tired."

"It's no wonder. I watched you and your sister work your magic earlier. I don't think you sat down once in the past five hours." He nodded towards the barn again.

"No." She smiled as she watched a few lights turning off in the massive building. No doubt, her sister would be locking everything up and heading down the pathway towards the cottage soon.

"What time did you start today?" he asked, shifting the pile of his clothes sightly.

"Five," she told him without thinking.

"Five this afternoon?"

"No." She shook her head and turned back towards him.

"Five in the morning? What on earth for?"

She laughed. "Who else was going to decorate? Make sure the flowers, the cake, and the decorations arrived and were in place on time?"

"Employees?" he offered.

Her smile slipped slightly. They had a few part-time employees. But so far, it was Kara and Robin's job to do most of the prep work. The money for employees was saved for waitstaff and cleaning crew.

She would love to have enough money to hire a few full-time employees.

"A few but I've found that when it really matters, there's no better person to handle the details than someone who is invested completely." She tilted her head and ran her eyes over his face. "Why the Coast Guard?"

He shrugged quickly and moved his eyes past her towards the building. "No particular reason. It was there. I was available." His eyes moved back to hers. "You know the drill."

"You went to school in... Portland, correct?" she asked, trying to remember what she'd heard about the man from his family and wishing she'd paid better attention when they'd talked about him.

"Yeah."

"For?"

"I ended up getting my associates." He again glanced past her shoulder, as if avoiding her eyes somehow mattered.

"In?" she asked.

"Applied Science." He shrugged. "You? Did you go to college?"

"No. I finished a couple college classes in high school, but since I always knew what I wanted to do, we jumped at the chance to buy this place and start our business after my grandfather passed and left us money."

"It seems to be doing well," he said.

She glanced back and noticed that all the lights were off, sending the old barn into full darkness. Glancing over, she saw the lights in the cottage turn on. She knew that her sister would be wondering where she was soon.

"Yeah. We're thankful. Most weekends from now until next spring are booked solid."

"Not bad." His eyes ran over her again slowly. "I'm sure your sister is going to start wondering where you are. I'll walk you to the cottage."

"No need," she said, but his eyebrows went up as if he was waiting for her to deny him. "Okay," she relented and started walking with him towards the cottage.

"Do you like it?" he asked after a moment of silence.

"My job?" she asked. When he nodded, she smiled. "I love it. You? Do you like working for the Coast Guard?"

"It keeps me out of trouble," he answered.

She chuckled. "Your mother says the same thing."

He chuckled, and the sexy sound of it warmed her. The night air had cooled her off to the point that she was chilled, and she wrapped her arms around herself.

"Here." He stopped and laid his jacket over her shoulders. "It's cooled off." He tucked his shoes and other items under his arm to lay his jacket over her shoulders.

Instantly, she was surrounded by his scent and the warmth of his jacket and his hands, which still rested on her shoulders.

"Thanks," she said as her entire body started shaking for a completely different reason. Why was it she kept getting lost in his blue eyes?

He dropped his hands and took a step back and then started walking again.

"So, why Pride?" he asked as the cottage came into view.

"Our parents fell in love here in Pride," she answered.

"Your parents?"

"Yeah, they were snowed in here one Christmas and ended up falling in love. Long story, but since then, we've come back here and stayed at the bed and breakfast once a year. Both Robin and I sort of fell in love with the town." She shrugged. "So, when it came time to pick a place to start our business, we chose Pride. I found the property and convinced Robin to take the leap with me."

They stopped on the large front porch of the cottage, under the dim light.

"Any regrets?" he asked her.

"None. Do you regret coming back home after college?"

His eyes moved to the front door, then shifted back to her. "You'd better get inside."

She arched her eyebrows. "You have a tendency to avoid answering questions you don't like."

He smiled down at her, and her knees went weak.

"It's home. Where was home for you? Before this?"

"We moved around for a while and settled in Portland

when I was ten." She wrapped her arms around herself while holding his jacket tight to her body for warmth.

"You'd better get inside. Get warm." He sat on one of the wicker chairs and dusted his feet off, then slid his legs into his pants. She watched his reverse striptease and felt her entire body vibrating with want. How could a man be even sexier dressed than undressed?

When he'd finished pulling on his dress shirt and buttoning it up halfway, he moved towards her.

"I'll need my jacket back," he said with a crooked smile.

"Oh." She swallowed and shook her head, clearing her mind as she removed the jacket and handed it to him.

It was then that she realized she was standing in front of him still dressed in only her bra and panties. She held her discarded dress up against her chest.

Deciding it wouldn't be wise to step into the cottage in her bra and panties, she shook her dress out and then pulled it on over her head.

When she finished dressing, she met his eyes and realized he'd watched her with as much interest as she'd watched him.

"Well, thanks again for saving me," she said, feeling shy suddenly.

His eyebrows rose slightly. "Again? I don't think you thanked me before." He moved slightly closer to her, and she caught her breath as his eyes once more moved down to her mouth.

"I didn't?" She almost whispered it.

"No." He was just a breath away now, and she quickly licked her lips, wondering what he would taste like.

Just when he moved closer, the front cottage door swung open, and Robin stood there in the bright lights, looking at them.

Kara jumped away from Conner quickly, thankful that she'd managed to put her dress back on in time.

"There you are," Robin said with a sigh of relief. Then her sister noticed Conner and stilled. "Oh." She smiled, and Kara knew instantly what Robin was thinking.

"Thanks again for walking me home," she said quickly, knowing full well she'd have a million questions to answer once she and Robin were alone.

"Any time." His eyes moved past hers to her sister. "Remember, it's never a good idea to swim after dark or alone." He nodded to Robin before turning around and stepping off the porch into the darkness.

"What was that all about?" Robin asked after she shut the front door.

"Nothing," she almost groaned. She tossed her heels down on the sofa and sat down next to them.

"You went swimming?" Robin asked, sitting across from her. Already, her sister had changed into a pair of sweats and a large college T-shirt.

"I needed to cool down and do some thinking," she admitted. Now that she was safe inside her home, she realized just how much danger she had been in. If Conner hadn't come along... She shivered and jumped up. "I'm going to take a hot shower," she said quickly before her sister could ask any more questions.

A few minutes later, standing under the hot spray, the tears started along with uncontrollable shaking. Hugging herself, she sat under the spray and thought that she might never go in the ocean again.

When she finally slipped under her blankets, wearing the warmest sweats and sweatshirt she had, her mind switched gears to Conner. How he'd looked at her. How he'd treated her. It went far beyond any attraction she'd felt before. Stronger and more powerful.

What was she to do with that? Was it something she could afford to act on?

The Jordans were some of the nicest people she'd met in town. But Conner, his other unmarried cousins, and his younger brother had a reputation.

She didn't have any issues giving them their perfect weddings but trying to date him... that was a completely different thing.

She couldn't afford to piss off the biggest and strongest family in the small town. What if she dated him and things didn't turn out? Could she and Robin afford to lose the largest family in town as clients?

Drifting off to sleep, she realized she was better off keeping away from any available Jordan. Especially Conner.

CHAPTER FOUR

Seeing pictures of his niece on his mother's phone, he tried to imagine what his own children would look like one day.

He had a standing date with his mother and his aunts, along with several of his cousins. They would all crowd into the local bakery, Sara's Nook, the first Saturday morning of each month and catch up. It wasn't as if they didn't see one another all the time, but at least once a month they made sure they were all together instead of just running around and bumping into one another somewhere in town.

"Can you believe she's already walking?" his mother said, looking down at the picture of Georgia Jordan.

His mother handed the phone back to Georgia's mother, Blake Jordan, who had married his cousin Matthew almost two years previous. Even though Georgia was currently sitting in a highchair next to her mother, everyone around the table still gushed over the short video of the girl taking her first steps.

Not that he didn't think little Georgia was absolutely perfect, but he didn't get the big deal. Kids crawled, then walked. Soon, he bet Blake and his cousin Matthew would be racing after the little girl who would, no doubt, be getting into everything.

He loved his family, really, he did, but lately, the monthly breakfast meetings had turned into more of a show-and-tell than a catch-up session.

And the fact was, he didn't have anything to be proud of. No photos on his phone to pass around. No great achievements. No new experiences to brag about.

"I saved Kara Jenkins the other night after the wedding," he blurted out before he had time to think about the storm of questions his words would cause.

"You did?" His mother's face changed, and her eyes grew narrow as she scanned his face. Instantly, he realized he'd stepped in it.

He guessed that his mother, all of his aunts, and even his cousins were now plotting out his future.

"Can you believe she went swimming after the wedding?" He cleared his throat. "I mean, who goes swimming after dark?" He shook his head and tried to play it off as just another rescue. He could tell by the look his mother was giving him that she wasn't buying it.

"Well." He stood up suddenly. "I'm..." He scanned his mind for any reason to leave and came up blank. He had the rest of the week off and had no commitments with anyone. "I'm going to head out," he finished.

"I'll walk you out." His mother stood suddenly as well.

"No need..." he started to say, but she narrowed her eyes, and he cleared his throat again.

"I hope you're not coming down with a cold," Riley said sweetly before turning to Lilly and whispering something to her, causing them both to giggle. That is how it had always been. The two cousins were closer than most siblings.

"I'm fine," he replied to her. "Later," he said to everyone

else. He waited for his mother to gather her purse and follow him outside.

"I don't like it that you've been swimming at night." His mother turned on him once they were outside. Her words caught him off guard. He'd been sure that she was going to try and set him up with Kara somehow.

He shook his head. "I don't, very often," he lied.

"Allen has been talking to your father. He says you're training at night." She sighed. "It has your father worried. You know how he lost his father and his hearing."

"Yeah." He shifted and leaned against his truck. "It was a boat accident, not an evening swim. Besides, it's not like I'm going to have much longer this year to enjoy them. It was pretty cold the other night."

His mother smiled slowly. "Kara's single."

He groaned and rolled his eyes and started to reach for the door handle.

"Indulge your mother for a moment." She reached for his arm, stopping him.

He stilled and then turned back around to wrap his arms around her.

Allison Jordan was still a very beautiful woman, even though he could see a few more gray hairs on her head.

Conner was tall like his father and even though his mother wasn't a short woman, he still towered over her. Resting his chin on the top of her head, he sighed.

"I know that lately you're unhappy," she said against his chest. "We just want to see you happy."

He closed his eyes and took a deep breath. He could smell fall and the soft subtle scent of his mother. Both of them were comforting to him.

"I'm getting there," he replied.

"You know," she said suddenly as she looked up at

him, "your brother might need some help today. They are supposed to break ground on the clubhouse. He could possibly use some encouragement." She nudged him in the chest. "Besides, he's been complaining about working with Rose again." His mother groaned, but then smiled again. "Those two have never really gotten along. Ever since they were children, they've been at each other's throats."

Rose Derby was a family friend. Her parents were very close with all of his family. Ric and Rob, or Roberta, Derby had a summer home in Pride and had spent so much time in Pride that everyone in town thought of them as locals. Rose Derby had grown up right along all of the Jordan kids.

It was true—for some reason Rose and Jacob were always at each other's throats.

Todd, Conner's uncle, had recently hired Rose straight out of college to design the hundred-and fifty-acre subdivision he was building on the land that he'd purchased recently. Parker Clark, Todd's son-in-law, was slated to take on all the construction since he was in the business of building homes. Jacob had been hired to oversee it all.

Rose and Jacob were having to work very closely together on the massive project, which would no doubt stretch over the next few years. Hidden Cove subdivision was going to be the first new subdivision in Pride in over three decades. It was due to help out with the current housing shortage in the area.

"Sure." He shrugged. "I'll head up there today."

"Good." His mother's smile was back. "Now, I've got to go meet your father. We're heading into the city today to meet Rose's parents."

He'd heard the story of how the Derbys had met his folks plenty of times. If it hadn't been for Ric Derby, his mother's art wouldn't be in such high demand, or so both of his parents said all of the time.

"Have fun." He kissed his mother's cheek and then watched her walk over to her car and drive away.

Glancing around the small town he'd grown up in, he knew that the main reason he was home was to give himself time to decide his next steps. Living in the city had been okay, but at times he'd struggled to get outside his shell. And, to be honest with himself, it hadn't felt like home.

This did. Seeing the same townspeople rushing around with their daily lives somehow made him feel part of something bigger than himself.

Jumping into his truck, he drove slowly through town, taking his time on his way up towards the new subdivision.

As he was passing his cousin Suzie's flower shop, All in Bloom, he happened to glance over and catch a glimpse of something bright red. Taking a moment, he turned and smiled when he saw Kara stepping out of the shop, her arms full of flowers. Pulling over, he jumped out of the truck to help Kara with the armload.

"Need any help?" he asked, reaching for the flowers.

Surprise crossed her face, then she slowly smiled before nodding and replying, "Sure, thanks."

"Where to?" he asked, looking around for her car.

She chuckled. "Down the street." She motioned half a block up the street where the slight turn-off for Sunset Weddings was.

"You're going to walk these all the way down there?"

"Are you trying to wiggle out of helping? Remember, you offered to lend a hand," she pointed out with a chuckle.

"You don't have a car?" he asked, clarifying.

"Don't need one when the flower shop is less than a block away." She started walking.

"A long block. How about we ride?" he said, motioning to his truck.

Her eyebrows shot up. "Sure, if you're offering. I have a few more loads." She nodded her head towards the shop.

"Sure. Feel free to load up." He walked over and set the box of flowers in the back of his truck.

When they were done loading the back of his truck with flowers, there was a slight sheen of sweat on his brow.

"You were going to walk all of these to your place?" he asked, looking at the bed of flowers.

"Yes." She smiled. "It's great exercise."

"Hit the gym instead," he suggested as he rushed to open the passenger door for her. He enjoyed the sound of her soft laughter as she slid into the truck.

She was right, it was a very short drive to the wedding venue. It seemed the moment he pulled out onto the street, he was turning into the driveway and parking lot that had been cleared for the massive venue.

"What are you going to do when it starts snowing?" he asked her as he parked and shut off the truck.

She glanced over at him and shrugged. "Walk faster."

"Don't you have a car?"

"Sure, Robin and I have old yellow." She motioned to where the old truck normally sat. The thing had more rust on it than the barn had last year before they'd remodeled. The other night there had been large hay bales and pump-kins scattered around the truck, as if it was set up for a photo shoot. He remembered that his cousin had taken pictures in front of the thing for her wedding, which in her words, completed the whole country wedding atmosphere.

"That thing that was sitting there the other night?" He motioned to the empty spot. "I thought it was a prop."

She laughed. "No, she runs. When we need her."

"You need a new truck or, better yet, a van to haul all of this stuff," he said after she climbed out and started unloading the flowers.

"Why? We're less than a block away from an amazing flower shop that your cousin runs," she reminded him.

"And I know for a fact that she delivers." He helped her unload the flowers and walk them inside the barn.

"There's no need to bother her workers when they have other deliveries." Kara shrugged. "Besides, I like the walk." She set the flowers down on one of the large circular tables.

He'd been in the barn several times for events since they'd opened up last year. This, however, was the first time he'd been in it when it was empty.

The sheer size of the place was almost intimidating. As was the massive chandelier that hung overhead.

Most of the large round tables had been moved aside and all the chairs sat upside down on the tables.

Kara walked over and flipped on a switch, flooding the dim barn with light.

"I can unload the rest, if you have someplace that you're supposed to be," she offered, looking at him sideways.

"I'm free." He hoisted another box of flowers out of the bed of his truck. He almost bumped into her since she was standing directly behind him.

"I've got these," he suggested as he picked up another box. "Don't you have to be setting these up?"

"Not yet. The event isn't until tomorrow afternoon." She took another armful and followed him back inside.

"Will these last?" he asked, running a finger over the white petals of a rose.

"Yes, we have a refrigerated room in the back they'll be stored in until I set out everything tomorrow."

He frowned. "Then why aren't we taking them back there?"

"I didn't want to put you out too much," she admitted.

He hoisted the box up and motioned. "Lead the way." As he followed her through the large space, past all the tables and chairs and the massive wood staircase that led to the second floor, he took in everything about the space. When he'd been there before, he'd been so focused on the people who had filled it.

He had no idea that behind the stairs there was a full-sized gourmet kitchen in the back. He hadn't thought about where all the food he'd enjoyed had come from.

"This is nice." He looked around the empty space.

"Yeah, Parker did a great job turning this into a kitchen." She turned to glance over at him. "It used to be stalls for pigs." She chuckled and turned back to the task of opening a large refrigerator door.

"It did?" He glanced around the space again and realized that the outer walls were newer than everything else in the place.

He wondered just how much the sisters had spent on fixing the place up and if they'd had work done on the cottage they lived in as well. He'd helped Stephan Roger move out of the old place and remembered thinking that whoever moved in to the place would need to put work into it to make it livable.

As he helped her cart the flowers into the back, he asked.

"So, did Parker fix up the cottage too?" He was surprised when she frowned.

"No, Robin and I are trying to do that work ourselves." She groaned.

"Why?" He remembered everything that he could about the cottage and its last state.

"We spent most of our funds fixing this place up." She set the last box of flowers into the refrigerator. "We both agreed that the business should come first," she added with a shrug.

"At least it's comfortable, right?" he asked.

She shrugged again and walked out of the kitchen. "We spend most of our time here."

He followed her out to the main area again and thought about spending his day following his brother around versus spending it helping Kara.

"I can help," he said quickly.

She turned back towards him, her eyebrows lifted slightly.

"With?" she asked after a moment.

He shrugged and felt like a fool.

"Whatever you need," he answered quickly. "My brother-in-law isn't the only one good with his hands."

CHAPTER FIVE

For just a split second, Kara's mind went to a vastly different place than she knew Conner's had been. Images of him hovering above her, pleasing her, flashed so quickly in her mind that she reached over and grabbed the edge of a table.

"You know, if you have painting or something like that that needs to be done in the cottage?" He shrugged and suddenly looked uncomfortable.

That instantly cleared those sexy thoughts from her mind. Though her body was still vibrating at the thought of him touching her and of her enjoying that sexy body that she'd seen the other night in the moonlight.

"I couldn't ask…" she started as she thought about all the work that had to be done at the cottage.

"I offered," he countered quickly.

"Why?" She shook her head, not fully understanding why he was offering his help.

Again, he looked uncomfortable as he avoided her gaze.

"It beats helping my brother out today," he answered with a shrug.

"I thought you and Jacob got along." She leaned against the edge of the table and crossed her arms over her chest. Everyone in town knew the Jordan clan was as thick as thieves.

Here, in the daylight, she could take her time and fully assess the man. Not that she hadn't before, but after the other night, she realized she'd never really given him a full chance.

He, of course, had the standard good looks that all the Jordan men had. He was probably the tallest out of all of them, though Iian Jordan did tower over everyone. She figured Conner was easily six-four or six-five.

His dark hair was a deal curlier than his younger brother's.

"We get along great," he said easily as his eyes met hers. "It's Jacob and Rose that don't get along. They fight like... well, siblings. The thought of getting between them while they work on this project scares me." He shivered clearly for show since he had a smile pasted on his lips. "Besides, if I tell my mother that I'm helping you fix up the cottage, she won't pressure me as much to moderate the fights I know are ensuing up at the job site."

"Jacob and Rose?" she asked, watching him closely.

"Rose Derby, a friend of the family. My uncle hired her fresh out of college as head architect to design the new neighborhood. As I said, she's like a sister to us."

"Jacob doesn't get along with her?" She couldn't imagine it. Jacob was easily the most outgoing Jordan man she knew. He was always laughing and joking about something.

Conner chuckled and leaned a little closer. "Riley's always joking they should just sleep together, then the fights would end."

Kara smiled. "I had wondered if he had someone."

Instantly, Conner's eyes narrowed as he leaned back.

Kara could tell that he was thinking she had an interest in his brother and for a moment thought about telling him she didn't. But something made her keep her mouth shut. She liked thinking that he was a little jealous. After all, that would mean that he had an interest in her. Right?

"If you want to help," she continued with a shrug, "we were going to pull up the old carpet. It stinks." She frowned. "It means pulling out all the furniture thought and, well, Robin and I haven't had the time or the energy."

"I'm your man then." His smile was back. "If you show me what you want done, I can start today."

"Today?" She thought of the mess she'd left in her bedroom and wondered about the rest of the place. Robin was the tidy one. Kara wasn't a slob, she'd just been busy that morning. Robin had taken the truck into Edgeview early that morning to get supplies, and Kara had been tasked with picking up the flowers today. Actually, the more she thought about it, it had been her only task. She'd expected the job to take several hours since she would be walking back and forth to the flower shop.

There were parts of her that wished she still had her old car, which she'd sold to pay for the new BlueStar platinum series natural gas range for the kitchens. Then she remembered that everywhere she had to go in town was within walking distance. Besides, they depended on that stove for the business.

"Sure, I mean..." Conner broke into her thoughts. "I'll have to head back and grab some tools first. If you want paint, I can swing by and grab that and some supplies." He was thinking out loud, which gave her more opportunity to watch him.

With the sunlight streaking into the building, she could see honey colored specks mixed in his blue eyes. She got so lost in looking at them that she lost track of his conversation and when he stopped talking, she had to blink a few times to try and catch up.

"Sure," she answered and started towards the door. "You can start in the living room. That carpet is the worst. We haven't picked out what we're going to replace it with, but at this point, exposed boards are better."

"Some of these old homes have hardwood underneath. The last time I was in the cottage—"

"You've been in there before?" She stopped on the pathway between the two buildings and he almost bumped into the back of her.

"Yeah, I knew the Rogers family. They had a son around my age. He left shortly after high school and joined the Marines."

"Of course." She started walking again. Everyone in Pride knew everyone. She should have thought of that before.

When they stepped through the front door, she glanced around with a slight groan. Yup, the place was a mess.

Conner instantly knelt inside the door and yanked the carpet back.

"Yup." He smiled up at her. "There's some nice hardwood under here. I bet we can sand it down and stain it and this place will look good as new." Then he glanced around. "How do you feel about the yellow walls?"

She winced. "Hate them. Both Robin and I were thinking of going with a light sky blue or a robin's egg blue." She walked over and grabbed the paint samples they had chosen.

Conner held them up and squinted his eyes as he looked around the room with them in front of his eyes.

"Sky blue." He held it up and then moved closer to her. "Squint your eyes and look between the color and the walls."

He was standing so close to her now that she could almost hear his heartbeat. She tried to focus on doing as he asked, but then his soft sexy scent filled her senses and her knees almost buckled.

"Okay," she said after a moment, not caring really what color the walls were just as long as the dirty yellow was gone.

"I'll head into town and pick up the supplies." He glanced around and tucked the paint sample into his pocket. "If you want to get the smaller items out of the room, I'll help you move the bigger ones into the dining area until the flooring and paint are done."

"Sure." She glanced around.

"You weren't doing anything else today?" he asked suddenly.

"No, thanks to you, my one job today is done," she answered with a smile.

His smile was quick. "Good." He turned towards the door, then stopped. His eyes ran over her slowly. "You may want to put on some work clothes. Even though you look great in it, I'd hate for your dress to get dirty."

She glanced down and nodded slowly.

When he walked out of the door, she slid onto the sofa and melted.

Damn. How could the simple look from him do that to her? She'd seen him around town for over a year and had hardly given him a second thought other than to recognize he was a sexy piece of meat. Now that he'd given her a little attention, her body was practically bursting into flames when he looked at her.

She fanned her face, and took a moment for the heat to leave her face. She got up and rushed around the room, tossing all their personal items into their own rooms.

Less than an hour later, when she heard Conner's truck pull up outside, she had everything removed from the living room except for the big furniture. She'd also changed out of her skirt and blouse into a pair of worn jeans and a tank top under the oversized sweatshirt she always wore when she painted or sketched.

Swinging the door open, she smiled and felt excitement grow when she thought about working with him to better the cottage.

"Wow, you work fast," he said, setting a bag of tools and a paint bucket just inside the doorway.

"I've been dying to fix up this place," she admitted. "I just didn't have the willpower to do it all myself."

He chuckled. "What about Robin?" He glanced around.

"She's running errands all day today. And trust me, she'll be fine with whatever we do to improve it in here." She motioned to the floor. "She hates having to wear shoes inside."

He nodded. "Think you can help lift the sofa? If not, we can slide it—"

"I can help," she jumped in.

"Okay." He motioned to one end. "We can fit it over by the table."

She'd already moved all the end tables and other small stuff herself into the dining area. The sofa and the two recliners were all that was left.

The moment everything was moved out of the room,

she stood back and watched Conner yank up the old carpet. It took him only a few tugs to have the massive square up from the floor and rolled into a heap. The amount of dust that floated in the air had her coughing and racing to open the front door and windows.

"Sorry," he mumbled. "I should have thought to ask you to do that before I started yanking this up." He bent down and lifted the entire carpet in his hands. "I'll take this outside."

Once all the windows were opened, she leaned down and started removing the carpet pad. Sure enough, a beautiful dark hardwood floor was underneath the mess.

"Here, let me help with that. If we do it right, we can roll it up easily," Conner said when he came back into the room.

They spent the next few minutes trying to get the pad up, but it had been stapled down to the hardwood floor with big staples. Conner disappeared outside and came back with a pair of pliers and started pulling out each spot that was stuck.

In the end, she had to bring in her large garbage can and stuff it completely full of the pieces of the padding, which were nothing more than hand-sized chunks by the time they were done.

She poured them each a glass of iced tea as Conner pulled off all the tack boards from around the perimeter of the room. The wood strips came up a lot easier than the staples had.

They drank their tea and looked at the flooring.

"This looks..."—she shook her head slightly— "amazing. I mean, it's like a hundred times better already."

"If you have a broom and dustpan, we can get all the dirt cleared up. Then we'll be able to see just how damaged the wood planks are and how much sanding and staining will need to be done."

"Sure." She set her tea down and disappeared into the kitchen. She opened the pantry door and cried out when the door shifted and started to fall towards her.

Strong arms reached around her and held the heavy thing up.

"This is dangerous," he said, stepping around her and removing the door completely.

"It's on the list to fix." She sighed and rolled her shoulders, then reached in and took out the broom and dustpan.

Conner was looking at the rusted hinges on the doorframe.

"I might have some new hinges in my truck," he said absently. After he leaned the large door against the countertop, he turned towards her. "Are you okay?"

"Yes, thank you." She tried not to look too affected by his chivalry and those muscles he'd used to lift the heavy wood door.

His eyes ran over her slowly before he nodded. "I'll run out to my truck."

The moment she was left alone in the kitchen, she melted against the countertop, almost tipping over the door again.

Could she get any more turned on at this point?

Sure, the house was now a complete mess and covered in a layer of dust from the carpet, but watching Conner work was one of the greatest pleasures in her life.

When he walked in with a small box in his hands, she was back under control. Or so she thought. When he started working on replacing the door, she excused herself and went back into the front room to sweep all the dirt and dust from the hardwood flooring. She even pulled out the mop and worked until the wood flooring almost shined.

She'd been so busy herself that she hadn't noticed that it had taken Conner a long time to rehang the door.

She stepped into the kitchen and held in a low gasp when she noticed he'd removed the cupboard doors.

"What are you doing?" she asked, instantly embarrassed at the lack of items and organization that the old doors had hidden. There had only been a few doors left on the cupboards when they'd moved in, and so they were the only cabinets that they had been able to use. The rest of the cabinets sat empty since they didn't want to showcase the mess.

"My mom has some cupboard doors that would go better in here," he said over his shoulder as he took down the last door. "She just had me move them all into the barn for storage. We can paint the cupboards and the doors and then add a few new knobs. By the time we're done, you'll have a new kitchen."

"I didn't expect you to go this far." She shook her head.

He looked concerned suddenly, and she reached out and touched his arm. "I'm thankful, but don't you have things to do other than this?"

He shook his head and then smiled quickly, and she felt her knees go weak.

CHAPTER SIX

How could he tell her that she was saving him? Saving him from having to follow his little brother around like an underling. It wasn't as if he didn't have skills of his own. Hell, he could outswim Jacob any day or night.

But in the last two years, Jacob had spent his free time getting his general contractor's license and studying everything there was to know about building.

"No, as I mentioned, I'm avoiding getting between my brother and Rose," he reminded her.

Her eyes narrowed slightly, and he understood she was skeptical of his reasoning.

He sighed and relaxed slightly. "About a year ago my uncle chose my little brother as head of what could be the largest project to come to Pride since the Coast Guard opened a training facility just outside of town about fifteen years ago."

Her eyes opened slightly. "It stings. Knowing that your sibling is..." She stopped talking when his eyebrows shot up.

"Smarter?" he asked. He knew that Robin took care of

the business side of things, while Kara tended to... be left hauling plants.

She frowned instantly and shook her head. "I was going to say more talented."

He chuckled and motioned around. "I'm pretty talented myself. At least when it comes to fixing things up. Our dad never let us go one summer without doing something constructive around the old place."

"Isn't your dad a chef at your family's restaurant?" she asked almost sarcastically.

He chuckled. "And I'm a glorified lifeguard."

"I wouldn't call you a glorified anything." She instantly closed her mouth, and he watched heat flood her cheeks.

He couldn't help but smile seeing her face heat. She'd been sexy in a dress at the wedding last week, damn hot in nothing but underwear and her bra as he'd pulled her from the water, but now, dressed in a pair of worn jeans and an old shirt covered in a layer of dust with her honey colored hair tied up, she was knockout gorgeous.

Clearing his throat to break the silence, he shifted and glanced out the window.

"What do you say we start painting the walls?" he offered.

She glanced back at the room and nodded.

Two hours later, they both stood and looked at the perfectly painted sky-blue room. The new color, mixed with the dark color of the wood, completely changed the room.

"It's hard to believe that I'm standing in the same room," Kara said. "I can't thank you enough for helping out."

He turned to her and reached up to brush a drop of blue paint from her face. He heard her breath catch when he moved closer. He hadn't counted on getting caught up in her eyes or the immense sudden desire to kiss her.

Her body swayed to his as her eyes moved down to gaze at his lips. He did the same and held in a groan at the thought of what she would taste like.

They both glanced towards the windows when they heard a car outside.

Seeing the old truck pull into the parking spot out front, he figured now was a perfect time to head out and grab the doors for the cabinets.

"I'll head on over to my place and grab the cabinet doors." He started to turn and then stopped. "I can be back after lunch with some other paint and the doors if you want to continue working in there."

Her smile was quick. "I'd love that." She followed him out to the front porch where her sister was unloading items from the back of the truck. "Thanks again for your help," she called after him brightly.

"Sure thing." He nodded to Robin as he passed her and headed to his truck.

He hadn't wanted to stick around long when he'd spotted Robin show up. He knew how sisters could be and figured it was better not be around to witness how Kara explained the destruction they'd caused in the place. Then again, with the new paint and the hardwood floors exposed, he knew it was just a matter of cleaning things up and putting it all back together before it would look amazing.

Driving back to the house, he decided to sidestep explaining to his mother why he'd skipped out on helping Jacob and headed directly to the storage barn where he'd stored all the old cupboards and all the other things his mother had made him haul out of the house over the past year.

He knew that at one point his mother had run her family antique shop in town. It could easily explain why his mother was always holding onto old furniture.

Stepping into the dim barn, he was slightly surprised to see his father rummaging through the drawers of an old dresser they'd moved out of the house less than a month ago.

Walking over, he waited until his father noticed him standing off to the side just in the corner view of his eye.

"What are you doing here?" his father used sign language to ask him.

"I'm taking the old cupboard doors to Kara's and maybe the buckets of French white paint mom decided was too bright for her office."

His father's dark eyebrows shot up as a slow smile formed on his lips. "Avoiding helping your brother out?"

Iian Jordan wasn't a difficult man to read. It probably helped that Conner was pretty much the spitting image of his old man and saw the same expressions in the mirror each day. The main difference was Conner's curly hair. Jacob had gotten his father's straight locks while Conner took a little more after his uncle Todd.

Conner rolled his eyes. "Don't start on me," he warned. His father's smile grew as he tilted his head slightly. "Mom has already complained that I'm not up helping Jacob. I think she wants me to be the peacekeeper between him and Rose."

His father's laughter echoed in the barn.

"Those two have been dancing around one another for years," his father signed then sighed heavily. "Help me find something. I don't know why your mom didn't clean out all the drawers of this old thing before we hauled it out here."

"What are you looking for?"

"An old family photo book," he signed before kneeling

and digging into a drawer. Conner took another drawer and scoured through the paperwork until he found a black leather-bound photo book underneath.

He tapped his father on the shoulder. "Is this what you wanted?"

He'd expected his father to look relieved, but he just nodded slightly.

"Go on, take a look." His nodded to the thing. "It was your grandfather's." His father leaned against the hutch and waited as Conner opened the book.

He couldn't remember seeing the thing before today, but some of the pictures inside were as familiar as his own face.

Larger prints of some of the images hung in the upstairs hallway in the house he'd grown up in. The house his great-grandfather had built when he'd moved to Pride with his young family and opened his restaurant, the Golden Oar.

Seeing several generations of men who shared the same features, the same eyes, as Conner had never really affected him. Until now. There were some images here he'd never seen before, and he couldn't help thinking about who the men in the pictures really were. What had their hopes and dreams been? Did they have the lives they'd wanted? Were they really in as much love as their smiles showed?

"That's George, my dad," his father said out loud, tapping the image Conner had been looking down at. "And Karna, my mother. The picture must have been taken just before I was born."

His father didn't speak often, but Conner had grown up knowing his voice well enough. He usually refrained from using it in front of anyone other than family.

Conner stared down at the couple. His grandmother was easily half the age of her husband. He knew that

George, his grandfather, had been married once before, to his uncle Todd's mother, who was still alive and living somewhere in California. He'd heard his uncle complaining several years back how the woman kept coming back to him to try and get money, but as far as he knew, the woman had never wanted to step into the role of mother or grandmother.

He knew the stories of Karna Jordan. How she'd met his grandfather on one of his trips to Norway and had fallen head over heels with the man, leaving everything behind to start a family. She'd taken Todd in and had been the first mother figure he'd ever known. She and his grandfather had several years of blissful marriage before she'd died in childbirth, giving her life for that of his father's. Just like George Jordan had on Iian's eighteenth birthday when he'd thrown Iian into a dinghy just as lightning had hit him and his boat.

"You look more like him than I do," his father said with a low sigh. "You know, I could have sworn I saw him once."

Conner jerked around and looked into his father's eyes to see if he was joking. His brother, Jacob, took after their father in that area. There wasn't a time he couldn't remember the two of them playing practical jokes on one another, or worse, on him.

But this time, Iian Jordan's eyes were filled with anything but laughter.

"When? Where?" he asked clearly so his father could read his lips, since he was still holding the photo book.

"In the hallway just outside our bedroom. The night I realized I didn't want to live without your mother." His father's lips twitched, then turned into a smile. "Your uncle found me face down, naked on the floor a few hours later." He chuckled.

Conner grew worried until his father's laughter registered.

"You know, Matt and Blake swear they've seen ghosts too." He nudged his father's shoulder.

"We all saw them that Christmas." His father sighed. "This was different." His smile slipped again. "All these years I swore I'd been concussed or..." He tapped his head. "It was something surfacing from my accident."

"Now?" he asked before looking back down at the image.

His father laid a hand on his shoulder and straightened up. "Bring it into the house with you when you come," he said instead of answering, he and started walking away.

That was one thing about having a deaf man in the house. When his father was done with the conversation, you couldn't really argue with him when he walked away.

He spent the next few minutes looking through the photo album, then he tucked it into the glove box of his truck. For the next half hour, he sanded down the old cupboard doors and dug through the barn for the buckets of paint he knew were out there.

When he walked into the large house that he'd called home all of his life, with the exception of the two years he'd spent on campus in Portland, his mother was standing in the kitchen, stirring something on the stove that smelled like heaven.

His father was standing behind her, his hands on her hips as he whispered something in her ear, which caused her mother to laugh.

"What are you cooking?" he asked as he set the photo book down on the bar top.

His mother glanced over her shoulder, which of course

got his father's attention. He still didn't pull away from his mother, though.

"Your father is cooking, I'm stirring," she corrected and sidestepped away from the stove as his father took over.

"Good," Conner joked as he sat down. "I thought it smelled too good for your cooking."

His mother chuckled and walked over to look at him. "Your father tells me you've been helping Kara out?"

"I have." He knew better than try to get out of telling his mother less than everything.

"I helped her carry some plants this morning after breakfast, and she asked me if I knew someone who could help her with a few repairs around the cottage. I figured it was the neighborly thing to do," he said with a shrug.

His mother had listened to him with a slight smile on her lips. Now, however, he could see the mischief growing behind her eyes.

"That's good. Your dad tells me you're using the old cupboards?"

"Just the doors. What's he making?" he asked, trying to distract her. "Smells like chili?"

"Chicken chili," she said, "and cornbread. You don't want to take the whole cabinets over there?"

"No, I figured we'd paint her cabinets and the doors with the paint you didn't like for your office. We tore up the old carpet and painted the living room a light blue. The way they have it decorated now, I figure it would complete the whole beach vibe they have going."

His mother was silent for a while. "I'd been meaning to stop by the cottage and see if they needed anything. I have a few pieces in the barn that they may want. I should plan on stopping by later this week."

"Mom." He stopped her and placed a hand over hers. "I'm just helping out."

"Of course, dear, as you said, it's the neighborly thing to do. Those girls have done such a wonderful job turning that old barn into such a beautiful venue."

"Yeah," he agreed, since he knew his mother had other reasons for stopping by Kara's place. No matter what he did now, his mother was plotting and matchmaking.

CHAPTER SEVEN

"What's going on?" Robin asked as she stepped into the cottage. "Did Conner do all this?"

Kara looked around and smiled. "Yeah. It looks a million times better, and I haven't even put the furniture back yet."

"Wow, thank god the yellow walls are gone. This looks amazing." Her sister glanced around. "And hardwood. I can take my shoes off." She smiled and did just that, putting her shoes by the front door. "We'll need a shoe rack now."

Robin started towards the kitchen, but Kara stepped in front of her.

"We aren't done in there," she warned, trying to block her path.

Her sister's eyes narrowed slightly, then she easily side-stepped around her and gasped when she noticed the lack of doors on the cupboards.

"He fixed the pantry door." Kara rushed over and opened the door easily. "See, it won't fall on us anymore."

"There are no more cupboard doors." Robin set the bag of groceries on the countertop.

"Yeah, but he's going to be back soon with new doors. We're going to paint them and have them back up today." She tried to sound excited to sell the idea to Robin.

Her sister surprised her by slowly turning around, then shrugging her shoulders.

"It's bound to be an improvement when you're done," she admitted.

"You aren't mad?" Kara asked, a little shocked.

"Is it costing us anything?" Robin asked, shoving a container of orange juice into the fridge.

"No," Kara replied with a slight shrug.

"Then I'm not mad," Robin said, continuing to put the groceries away. "But don't expect me to help out. I have a pile of paperwork that I've been putting off and have to get done tonight."

"No." Kara shook her head quickly. "I think we can handle it."

"Good, then I'm going to have some lunch, then take my laptop over to the office in the barn and work until things are back to normal around here."

"Sounds good," Kara agreed with a smile.

One cold turkey sandwich and a bowl of grapes later, she got to work on mopping and shining the wood floor. The thing was in such great shape that she doubted it needed to be sanded. But she wanted to wait and get Conner's opinion before returning all the furniture to the room.

Robin gathered her things and disappeared out the front door to head over to the office at the barn ten minutes before Conner knocked on the door.

"We can paint the doors outside. I brought some sawhorses so they can dry while we paint the cupboards," he greeted her when she answered the door.

"Sounds good." She motioned to the living room. "Do

you think the floor needs anything but a good shine?" she asked him as she waved towards the floor.

"Wow, that cleaned up nicely." He stepped past her and bent to examine the flooring. "No, a nice coat of floor sealer should do the trick. Of course, you can do that at any time. It will take a full day or so to dry before you can put the furniture or rugs over it."

She frowned. "I may have to wait on that until next weekend. I doubt Robin will let me keep this place in such a mess for that long. We have the Garrett's wedding tomorrow, then the Johnson's anniversary party the following night, followed by..."

Conner held up his hand to stop her. "I got it. You're busy. So, we get as much done today as we can and return your place to normal."

"I hope we'll have it looking better than normal." She smiled. "I mean, the floor and the paint are a massive improvement. I feel like I can already remove my shoes." She frowned slightly remembering the carpet in her bedroom. "At least in here."

His dark eyebrows shot up. "You know, if my memory serves me right, the hardwood floor runs throughout the entire house. Except for the kitchen, dining room, and bathrooms, I mean."

"Oh, hardwood flooring in my bedroom." She sighed. "That would be a dream come true. Okay, next weekend we conquer removing the rest of the carpet throughout the house." She shook her head. "I mean, if you're free?"

"Something tells me that if I don't continue to help you out, my mother will skin me alive," he said as he stepped out the front door.

"Oh?" She noticed that he'd laid the doors on the sawhorses and had the paint sitting on the back gate of his truck along with paint supplies. "Your mother doesn't seem like the nagging type."

He chuckled. "She normally isn't, unless it has to do with meddling in her children's love lives."

Kara lost her footing on the last stair of the porch and almost ended up with her face planted in the small flower bed near the foot of the walkway.

Feeling Conner's strong arms wrapped around her again was intoxicating. Just the way he lifted her up and righted her until her feet were once again solid on the pathway was as sensual as any dance move that she'd ever witnessed.

"Easy," he said in a low tone as his hands remained wrapped around her waist.

"I'm a klutz," she heard herself blurting out. His soft chuckle had her slamming her mouth shut to ensure that nothing else stupid came out.

"Believe it or not, Jacob is the klutz in our family." He dropped his hands from her and took a step back. "Everyone always assumes it's Riley, not that she doesn't have her moments, but growing up, Jacob was the most likely to fall in a well or get his head stuck in the fireplace." He chuckled. "Which he did when he was six." He held up his fingers. "Twice."

She relaxed her guard and laughed. "I can totally see that. He tripped at the wedding and, if it hadn't been for your dad, he would have taken out the wedding cake."

Conner laughed again and then moved over to the cabinet doors. "These are pretty standard sizes. I compared them with the old ones I removed, and they should fit perfectly. Of course, we'll want to paint the cabinets as well before we hang these back up."

She focused on the doors and realized that they were

almost brand new. Once they painted them, they would make the entire kitchen seem new.

"They're perfect," she told him.

"Let me know if the color is off." He walked over and motioned to a can of paint. "There's plenty of it. My mother had me get three cans of it for her office, then decided she wanted soft teal walls instead." He smiled as if remembering something.

"I've heard all about your mother's workspace from your sister." She took up a paint brush and wiggled it. "So, where do we start?"

Four hours later, her back hurt, her right shoulder and elbow were sore, she had blue and cream paint in her hair and all over her clothes, and she was starving. Still, working next to Conner made her forget all of those little pains.

"We'll have to let everything dry for an hour," Conner said, standing back and setting his paintbrush in the bucket of water. "What do you say we head to the Oar and grab a burger?"

She glanced down at her ruined tank top and jeans.

"Trust me, you're dressed fine for a Thursday night at the Oar." He motioned to his own shirt with a few paint splatters on it.

"You're not half as messed up as I am." She motioned between their clothes. "Give me a few minutes to change and it's a deal." She started walking towards her room.

"I'll clean up," he said as she disappeared down the short hallway.

Once locked behind her bedroom door, she quickly assessed the damage and determined she needed a quick rinse in the shower. She piled her hair in a messy bun on top of her head and quickly rinsed off. After reapplying the basics in makeup and pulling on a dark pair of jeans and a clean T-shirt, she let her hair down and realized it looked better up.

When she walked out to the living room, she was happily surprised to see that he'd moved the rest of the furniture back into place.

"You'll want a few area rugs to protect the flooring after you seal it," he said before turning around. Then he noticed her, and he smiled. "Now I feel like I'm underdressed."

She chuckled. "It's just jeans and a T-shirt."

He shook his head. "You look beautiful."

She caught her breath as he closed the step or two that was between them. Then, before she had a moment to prepare, he gathered her in his arms and kissed her.

Since the other night, she'd dreamed of what it would be like to be kissed by him. How his body would feel next to hers. How his lips would taste.

It wasn't as if she'd had a lot of experience before now. She'd dated a few boys in school, but Conner was the first man.

Her entire body began to shake and feel slightly uncomfortable, so she pulled back.

"I've wanted to do that since the other night when I rescued you," he admitted.

She held her breath for a moment and before she could think of a reply, she blurted out, "You didn't rescue me."

His smile doubled. "Sure." He reached down and took her hand in his. "Let's take this argument to the restaurant. I'm starving."

CHAPTER EIGHT

Sitting across from Kara at one of his favorite places in the entire world seemed almost surreal. He was not only surrounded by familiar smells, sights, and sounds but knew everyone in the restaurant, both employees and customers.

He didn't have to even glance at the menu and, instead, took the time to assess Kara as her eyes moved over the dinner options.

"What's your favorite?" she asked him after a moment.

"Everything," he admitted.

She chuckled and set her menu down. "Then order for me. I can't decide. It all looks amazing."

He nodded and waved Carrie over.

"Hey, Conner." Carrie smiled down at him before turning to Kara. "Evening."

"Carrie, you remember Kara? She and her sister, Robin, run Sunset Weddings." He introduced the two.

"Right." Carrie's smile grew. "Where were you guys when Josh and I got married a few years ago?" she joked. "I hear you guys are booked solid now?"

"Almost." Kara seemed to relax. Then she shook her head slightly. "You're married to a cop. Right?"

Carrie chuckled. "No, Aiden's the only cop in my family now and he's my brother."

"Oh, right. We just did his and Suzie's wedding last week," Kara said.

"It was an amazing wedding. They're off on their honeymoon in Europe all this week." Carrie smiled, then added, "I'm married to Josh. He helps me run Carrie's Sanctuary. I occasionally help out here when needed." She shrugged. "I started working here in grade school," she joked.

"Right." Kara snapped her fingers. "You own the amazing animal sanctuary just outside of town. I've been meaning to head out there. Not that I can afford to bring anything home with me, but..." She shrugged. "I can look."

Carrie nodded. "Speaking of knowing what you want, have you guys decided?"

"Two of tonight's specials," Conner responded.

"Great choice. I'm taking a few specials home when I get off shift." Carrie wrote down their orders and added their drinks and left.

Conner leaned across the table and lowered his voice. "A little hint; always order the special. It has never steered me wrong when I don't know what I want."

"Good to know. I've had lunch here plenty of times, but not dinner yet." Kara glanced around. "For some reason, I was thinking people would waltz in here in formal attire."

He held in a chuckle. "Only on Saturdays."

Her eyebrows shot up and he could tell that for a split second she believed him. Then she relaxed and shook her head as she continued to look around.

"I hear that your great-grandmother painted most of

these." She motioned to the large oil paintings covering the walls.

"Yes." He smiled and followed her gaze. "The mermaid is everyone's favorite."

"That's your mother's." She motioned to a painting of a small boat.

"Yes." His smile slipped a little. "The Dawn-Treader." He sighed. "It's my mother's gift to my dad." His eyes met hers. "It's the sailboat he and my grandfather were in when my dad lost his hearing and George Jordan lost his life."

"I'm so sorry. It's still a lovely painting," she said softly. "And my favorite in here."

His full smile returned. "My father proposed to my mother standing right there, in front of that piece."

Kara's eyebrows shot up, and she glanced at the art again. Then she slowly smiled, and he could see her eyes soften.

"How wonderful." She practically purred it. The low sound caused his body to vibrate with want.

He'd meant the kiss he'd given her to be light. He'd wanted to taste her from the moment he'd pulled her out of the water, but he hadn't expected to be hit by a lightning flash of desire when she'd responded in his arms. Even now, he wanted to taste her again. Wanted to feel her soft body up against his.

He tried to focus on their conversation during dinner, but his mind and his body kept returning to that kiss. Even though he was gloriously tired from the long day's work, he still had the energy to climb a mountain if he knew he'd be rewarded with another kiss from Kara.

It was stupid. He was stupid. He knew his heightened libido was due to the fact that it had been a few months since he'd been out on a date. Longer than that since he'd been with anyone. Sure, he knew the rumors going around town about the Jordan men. Some of them were true, others weren't.

He wasn't like his cousin George, who had a different woman on his arm or in his bed each time he talked to him. Out of all the Jordan men, George was the biggest player.

The running family joke was that it would take a freight train to tie George down. That or a woman that could knock him on his ass and hog-tie him.

"You're deep in thought," Kara said as he drove them back to the cottage.

He chuckled. "Thinking about my cousin George." He shook his head.

"Which one is he again?"

For some reason this made him laugh even more. "Probably the one who's hit on you." He glanced at her. "Multiple times."

Her eyes narrowed, as if she was trying to remember all the Jordan men.

"Not married?" she asked.

He laughed harder. "No," he said between the laughter.

"Lighter brown hair? Haunting silver eyes?" she asked slowly.

"Yup, that's the one."

She smiled as he parked beside the old truck.

"He hasn't hit on me," she said, surprising him.

Shutting off the truck, he turned to her. "He hasn't?" He frowned and ran his eyes over her as she shook her head from side to side slowly. "Why the hell not?"

This time it was her laughter that filled the cab of the truck. "Guess I'm not his type?"

"Every woman is his type," he responded quickly.

"Now, your bother on the other hand..." she began, and he felt his entire body stiffen.

"What?" He almost growled the word out.

She lifted her shoulders slightly in a shrug.

"He asked me to dance at your cousin's wedding," she said, glancing over at the small cottage.

"Did you dance with him?" he asked between clenched teeth.

Her eyes moved back over to his, and the corners of her mouth curved up.

"Why? Are you the jealous type?" she whispered.

His eyes moved to her lips, and he watched her tongue slowly play over her bottom lip. He hadn't realized he'd groaned out loud, but when her eyes darted to his lips, he reached for her. He came up short when his seatbelt jerked his shoulder back.

The soft chuckle of hers had him groaning at his stupidity.

Yanking off his seatbelt, he reached to undo hers and then pulled her across the space until she was pressed up against him.

"Normally, no," he said, cupping her chin with his fingers. "But the thought of you dancing with my little brother irritates me."

Her smile grew. "I turned him down. Employees aren't supposed to dance with guests."

He relaxed slightly and ran his eyes over her face slowly.

"I'd like to kiss you again," he said softly.

"I'd like that," she whispered. She leaned into him as her hands moved over his shoulders.

She tasted better than before, felt better than before. Her entire body melted against his. His hands roamed over her hips, her back, as she lightly dug her nails into his shoulders.

When the porch light flashed on, Kara jerked free of his hold and sighed.

"I'd better go." Her eyes were glued to the cottage.

"I'll come in and hang the doors. They're bound to be dry by now." He got out before she could say no. He raced around the truck and helped her out, and they walked into the cottage together in silence.

Robin was sitting on the sofa, engrossed in a book. Or so it appeared. When they walked in, she glanced up and smiled at him.

"Evening," she said in a soft tone.

"Hi." He nodded to her. "I'll get these doors hung and get out of your hair," he told them.

"Thank you," Robin said. "The place looks so different." She set her book down. "I guess it was lucky that Kara ran into you today and lucky that you had time to help out."

He felt Robin's eyes running over him, assessing him.

"She helped me avoid helping my brother out," he said with a shrug before turning and disappearing into the kitchen.

"Wow," Kara said after he'd hung the first door up. "They look brand new."

He had to admit that the cabinets looked amazing. "I didn't have one that would fit this one above the refrigerator, but I figured I could take measurements and cut one down. I can drop by later this weekend to hang it."

"I'm just thankful we have more than a few cabinets we can use." She was sitting on the edge of the countertop, helping him hang the next door. She held it in place while he used his drill to screw the new hinges into place.

"You're lucky to have granite countertops. Patty sells

some granite polish down at the grocery store. I bet you can get it shining like new."

"I'll stop by tomorrow and get some before the event." Kara dropped her hold on the next door as he finished up. "I'm sure we can make it without..." she started.

"It's no problem. I like to finish a project. Besides, something tells me that my mother will be stopping by later this week to check out my progress." He rolled his eyes with humor. "You might actually get a visit from all my aunts."

She chuckled. "The perks of having a big family."

"Oh? Do you have a large family?" he asked.

She chuckled. "No, not really. My father was an only child and best friends with my mother's only brother." She held the next door as he got to work.

"My uncle Todd was best friends with my aunt Megan's brother, before he died," he said absently.

Kara sighed. "It's one of the reasons why we picked Pride to open our business. The fact that this is where our parents fell in love." She glanced towards the dark kitchen window. "Coming here every summer, we both decided it was one of the most romantic places we knew."

He stilled. "Pride? Romantic?" He chuckled and shook his head as he got back to work.

"Of course, you won't think so. You were raised here. You're too close to the subject." She nudged his shoulder. Then she sighed and glanced out the window again. "But every wedding we've hosted so far says differently. The sunsets on the beach, the way we've turned the barn into a venue to make dreams come true."

Her voice had turned soft, wishful sounding. He stopped working and watched her closely as she spoke. She probably didn't realize how dreamy she sounded. How wishful.

"I never imagined it would turn out so perfect." She turned back towards him. When she realized he was watching her, she shook her head quickly and turned back to the task.

He'd never known anyone as committed to her dreams as Kara was. Well, with the exception of his cousin and sister. When they'd gotten it in their mind to open their boutique a few years back, nothing could have stopped them.

By the time he was finished hanging the last door, Kara had hidden a few yawns from him by covering her mouth with her hands.

"I've taken enough of your day," he said, gathering his tools.

"Are you kidding?" She leaned against the countertop. "You've saved us. You've single-handedly turned this place into a home in one day." She glanced around. "We were afraid to cook in here, for fear that the cabinets would fall off the walls."

He nodded. "The new screws I put in place should hold up for years."

"See." She motioned towards him. "You saved us." She quickly stood up. "We owe you." Then she snapped her fingers. "Dinner."

His eyebrows shot up. "We've already had dinner," he reminded her.

"No." She waved her hand. "I mean, I owe you dinner. Properly." She glanced around. "Here."

"Okay," he agreed quickly.

"A week from now. Next Thursday?" she asked after glancing down at her phone.

"Okay," he agreed again, causing her to smile.

"You're easy," she joked, setting down her phone.

"When it comes to a free meal, what guy isn't?" he said with a chuckle.

She nodded. "Thanks again." She looked around just as Robin walked into the room.

"Wow." Robin could have easily been Kara's twin. They were almost identical except that Kara's hair was a few shades lighter than Robin's and Kara's smile and eyes drew him in and did things to his gut and his loins. "This looks amazing." She walked over and opened a door. "They all work now."

He nodded. "I'll bring the last two for above the fridge when I come on Thursday," he said to Kara.

"Perfect." She beamed before turning to Robin. "I'm making Conner dinner to thank him for all of this." She motioned to the cabinets and then to the hardwood floor and the living room walls.

"I didn't really do anything to the floor except yank up the carpet," he said.

"It looks like a different place," Robin said easily. "Thanks."

He nodded as he gathered his tool bag under his arm. "I'll leave you two to fill the cabinets. Night."

He walked out and put his tool bag in his truck. He tossed his sawhorses in the back and reached for the passenger door, only to stop when Kara called out his name.

Seeing her standing in the soft porch light, he caught his breath at her beauty. Why, oh, why hadn't he really noticed it before now?

He swallowed the desire that had rushed through him.

"Yeah?" he asked.

"You forgot." She waved his cell phone, which he'd left on the counter. He walked over and stopped at the foot of the porch steps. From here, they were eye to eye. He couldn't stop from gazing down at her lips as he took the phone from her, letting his fingers brush over hers slowly.

"Thanks," he said.

Before he could turn away, she jerked closer and covered his mouth with hers in a quick kiss.

"Night," she said. Before he could respond, she turned and rushed back into the house.

Smiling, he climbed into his truck and ignored the tiny voice in his head screaming that he was in deep trouble.

CHAPTER NINE

A bead of sweat trickled down the middle of Kara's back. How could the evening be so humid? Wasn't winter supposed to be right around the corner? The leaves on all the trees had already changed colors, yet only a few had hit the ground so far.

It was easily hotter tonight than it had been at their last event. Maybe it was because she had been forced to run around and replace all of the decorations after one of the guest's children had pulled down most of the ones she'd put up earlier that morning.

The wedding the evening before had been perfect, but this anniversary party seemed to be going less smoothly.

It didn't help that she'd had a tough time sleeping last night. The night before she'd been so tired after the full day's work that she had fallen into a deep dreamless sleep. But last night her mind and her dreams had been filled with Conner.

Normally that would be a good thing, but she'd ended up only having five hours of sleep before she had to wake up and get ready for a birthday party lunch then switch the decorations for the evening's anniversary party.

"We really need to hire a few more employees," Robin said in passing.

"Yes," she agreed as she rushed the opposite direction. "Hopefully, before next weekend." She disappeared into the kitchen for more tape.

When she didn't find any extra tape rolls in the kitchen, she darted out the back door, knowing there were four new rolls in one of the cottage's kitchen drawers. She'd put them there herself the other night when returning her kitchen to normal after Conner had left. She and Robin had spent most of the night reorganizing the cabinets and drawers.

Their kitchen now looked as if it could be in the country magazines she always browsed through at the market.

She hadn't been watching where she was going and bumped solidly into a very large dark mass.

"Oh, I'm sorry," she said, thinking it was a guest.

"Miss Jenkins?" The older man gripped her shoulders as if to hold her in place. She frowned and instantly wished that there were lights on the pathway between the cottage and the barn.

"Yes? Can I help you? Are you a guest?" she asked, a little breathless.

"No, I'm a lawyer." The man continued to hold her shoulders. "I'm here about this property."

Kara's heart jumped in her chest and then did several little flips. Everything had gone smoothly with the closing more than a year ago, but at the possibility that something was wrong, her head felt light.

"Is there a problem?" she asked, tensing.

Instead of answering, the man took a deep breath, and,

in the darkness, she could imagine him assessing her before he finally spoke. "There could be. I'm here because my client would like to make an offer on some of your land."

She relaxed instantly and held in a chuckle. "We're not interested." She moved to sidestep around the man, but he continued to hold onto her shoulders.

In the year that she'd lived there, not once had she felt unsafe. Even walking on the dark pathway between the cottage and the barn or on her many walks on the dark beach at night. Now, however, with the large man hovering over her, holding her in place, she felt panic start to bubble in her gut.

"That's just the thing. I think this offer is one you and your sister might not want to overlook," the man said in a deep voice.

"If you could come back during business hours"—she tried to break free from his hold— "maybe my sister and I could entertain your client's offer. However, currently, we are in the middle of an event and I'm running late."

When she finally got free of the man, instead of continuing down the pathway towards the empty cottage, she turned around and rushed back through the kitchen door of the barn.

Leaning against the barrier, she took several deep breaths.

"You okay, missy?" Joy, their head cook, rushed to her side. "You're as white as the biscuit dough I'm rolling." The woman gripped her shoulders, much like the lawyer had outside. Only Joy's touch was soothing instead of nerve-racking.

"There was a man," she started, closing her eyes and trying to swallow the panic.

"Where?" Joy's voice turned from concern to anger.

"No." Kara sighed. "He was a lawyer," she corrected. "He... had an offer..." She rolled her eyes. "I guess he just spooked me because it's dark out there and... well, he caught me off guard."

Joy's eyes narrowed as she glanced towards the back door. "Did you get the lawyer's name?"

"N-no," she admitted. She'd been so eager to get away from him that she hadn't even thought to ask him.

"I'll have Will go out and see if he can find the man." Joy turned and waved to one of the waitstaff. Will happened to be the largest of the men that worked for them.

Before Kara could convince Joy that she'd just overreacted, Will was heading out the back door looking for the man.

She sat inside the kitchen and drank the glass of water Joy offered to her as they waited. Moments later, Will returned and shook his head.

"The pathway was empty. Only a few guests in the parking lot. The rest are out on the patio or inside here. Could he have come inside?" he asked.

"No, I don't think so. I'll make my rounds and double-check. Thanks," she said to both of them. Now that she was back under control, she added putting in pathway lights to her to-do list.

Forgoing the tape, she reapplied the decorations that had been pulled down earlier. She made her way through the entire barn and outdoor patio area and didn't run into the lawyer again. Thankfully.

By the time the last guest had left, she'd convinced herself that she'd overreacted due to lack of sleep and asked Robin if she would oversee the cleaning.

She knew that the following day they had a tea meeting for a group of churchgoers shortly after noon. They'd played host to the women's group from the moment they'd opened their doors a little over a year ago.

She rushed down the dark pathway and was breathless when she locked the cottage door behind her.

She turned on every light and used up the rest of her energy cleaning her room.

When Robin walked in a little over an hour later, Kara collapsed on the bed and fell fast asleep.

The next morning, she was still dragging as she opened up the barn for the women's group. It was by far the easiest event to set up for. The group of twenty to thirty women only used the coffee maker and several tables. They tended to bring baked goods and always shared with Kara, even though she never stuck around for the entire event.

Not that she wasn't religious, but the ladies were from the local Catholic church and she'd been raised attending a Baptist church.

Still, she knew most of the women by their first names at this point and often ran into them in town. It was nice growing familiar with the locals.

There wasn't a time she didn't bump into someone she knew and enjoy a quick chat. It made her feel almost important somehow.

This morning, however, after taking a large maple bar and a to-go coffee, she walked out on the beach and sat in the soft sand to think.

It wasn't often she had moments like this to relax. Most of her week was spent getting things ready for the weekends —ordering flowers and decorations or meeting with couples and showing off the venue. It was a delicate dance they had going, and she wanted to make sure everything stayed fine-tuned.

Robin usually spent her time scouring over receipts,

invoices, and spreadsheets, something Kara would never willingly sign up for.

It was strange, her entire life her parents had instilled the belief that the two of them could do whatever they set out to do. So, it's what both Robin and Kara believed.

They hadn't thought twice about starting their own business. Sure, they'd hashed out all the financial details and logistics of the business, but for the most part, the moment they'd decided it was possible, they'd been all in.

Unlike some of her friends she'd grown up with, she had never had to fear for anything. Her parents weren't incredibly wealthy, but they'd had enough money and love that Kara had grown up knowing she was secure in life, no matter what path she chose.

Yet, Conner's words had hit her the other night. It wasn't as if she lived in Robin's shadow, per se. But growing up, she'd known full well that Robin was the brains in the family.

Maybe this was why Conner's words about how he felt about his brother had hit her so hard.

She loved her sister as much as she could. They'd rarely argued growing up and, even now, they never disagreed about anything.

Okay, there had been a few times last year, after opening the business, when she'd lost a receipt or had forgotten to tell Robin about an expense. But they'd worked it out and now had a new system that was foolproof.

She couldn't imagine what Conner felt about the success of his little brother and sister. Everyone in town knew that Riley's store, Classy and Sassy, was one of the most successful boutiques around. People drove all the way from Portland to shop there.

Now the talk of the town was how Jacob and Rose

Derby were overseeing the construction of Pride's newest subdivisions. Townspeople drove up to the property on the weekends just to see the progress of the neighborhood. Every time Kara stepped into Sara's Nook, the local bakery and coffee shop, people were talking about the progress of the new subdivision and how proud the Jordans must be of Jacob.

"I was told I would find you out here." A woman's voice broke her out of her deep thoughts. Glancing back over her shoulder, she saw Allison Jordan walk gracefully across the sand towards her.

The woman had a pair of shoes in her hands and her pant legs were rolled up as if she belonged on the beach. Actually, Conner's mother could easily have just stepped off the big screen. The woman was so beautiful that Kara had found it difficult to believe she hadn't made a career in movies instead of art. She reminded her of Aubrey Hepburn in not only her grace but her beauty.

Kara started to get up out of the sand, but Allison stopped her.

"No, don't get up. If it's okay, I'll join you."

"Sure." She motioned to the sand. "Help yourself."

"Thanks." Allison tossed her shoes down and easily sat next to her and glanced out at the water. "It never gets old. Does it?" she said with a sigh as she rested her elbows on her bent knees.

Kara followed Allison's gaze out over the water and sighed.

"No," she agreed. "You always wonder what people who live near the ocean think of it. If they get tired of seeing it," she added, feeling a little foolish.

Allison chuckled softly. "Some do, I suppose. Or at least grow dull to its beauty." Allison's eyes turned back to Kara.

"Artists, on the other hand, well, we're a different breed. Aren't we?"

Kara's eyebrows rose slightly at being added into the same mix as the woman who sat next to her.

"Oh, don't be fooled." Allison chuckled. "I can spot an artist when I see one. After all, I've attended more than one of your wonderful events. You may not paint with a brush like I do, but what you create is still a masterpiece."

Kara's heart did a funny little flip.

"I've never really thought of it like that before," she admitted.

Allison sighed and nodded behind them. "It's the number one reason your business is flourishing." She turned towards her. "So, enough pleasantries. I'm here to see your cabinets," Allison said with a smile. "I'm dying to see what you've done with the cottage."

CHAPTER TEN

Conner had heard that his mother had gone over to the cottage to assess Kara and the work they'd done on the place. But his workweek had kept him too busy to worry about what his mother had said to Kara. Or what Kara had thought of the visit. He knew that some women put more stock than others in a guy's mother showing up for no real reason.

On Conner's next full day off, Jacob had specifically asked for his help. Which meant that he was stuck sitting in the construction trailer listening to Rose and Jacob argue about whether the clubhouse should have four tennis courts or two.

After almost five minutes of listening to them, he stood up. "Why not just meet in the middle and have three courts?" he suggested.

The two of them looked at him as if he'd grown a second head.

"That's a bad idea," Jacob said at the same time that Rose said.

"That's a terrible idea."

"See." Conner waved his hands. "There. At least you agree on that." He stalked out of the trailer. A blast of cool air hit him and, without thinking, he took off down the pathway to where the majority of the construction was taking place.

Currently, there were large machines plowing through the dirt, carving the pathways that would become the roadways through the neighborhood.

The Jordans were known for shipping, his mother's art, and the family restaurant. This was the first time the family was dipping their toes into construction. Sure, they'd remodeled or fixed places up over the years, but they'd never built anything from scratch.

He knew it was one of the reasons his brother had decided to go into the construction field. Each summer their dad had picked a project to work on, and Jacob had been right there, eager to get his hands dirty.

Not that Conner didn't enjoy seeing something fixed up and made new, like Kara's kitchen. He just didn't have the drive his little brother did.

Even working for the Coast Guard, he still felt... dull inside. The last time he'd felt alive, truly alive, had been when he'd kissed Kara.

Damn. He ran his hands through his hair and headed up the trail to the top of the hillside. He didn't know exactly where all the property markers were, but he figured that he could make it to the top of a small bluff. Maybe the hike would cool him off and give his brother and Rose time to settle the silly argument so they could get back to work.

His schedule at the Coast Guard didn't usually bother him, but lately, he wished his days off could be his. His family had been stepping in and making requests of him when they knew he had days free.

Forty-hour weeks weren't hard when he liked the work he was doing. But that didn't mean he didn't want some time to himself.

He thought about the day he'd spent with Kara and smiled. What he wouldn't give to spend a few more days like that. Kara was easy to get along with. She was light-hearted and laughed easily, something he found totally sexy in a woman. Not to mention the little tempting dimple near the corner of her mouth that flashed when she laughed. There was such a spark in her eyes when she was passionate about what she was talking about.

By the time he reached the top of the hillside that over-looked Pride and the beach far below, he was no longer agitated at his brother and Rose. His eyes scanned the tree-tops for a glimpse of the barn's rooftop.

Would it be weird if he stopped by tonight? His shoul-ders slumped. "Yeah," he answered out loud. He turned away from the view to head back down the hill and help his brother out for the last day off from work that week.

He'd just have to wait until tomorrow evening to enjoy being with Kara again. For the rest of the day, he worked his frustration off by helping pull one of the worker's trucks from the mud. In the past three days, it had rained enough to turn even the strongest hillside into a muddy mess. Which is why he'd left his truck parked on the main road.

It took several hours, and it didn't finally break free from the mud until they solicited the help of one of the bulldoz-ers. By then, he was covered in a thick layer of dark Oregon mud and he was dead tired.

Driving home, his mind kept returning to Kara's last kiss. He should have gotten her phone number so he could text or call her. Damn.

He thought of stopping off at his cousin's flower shop to

pick up a bouquet of flowers before he headed over there tomorrow evening.

He was passing the barn on the edge of his parents' drive, which used to house horses and a few cows, and, after seeing the light, pulled to the side of the drive and shut off the truck. He walked over, thinking that his mother was searching through the stuff they'd stored there. Instead, he stepped into the dark barn and was hit with a wave of Kara's sexy scent.

Leaning against the doorway, he crossed his arms over his chest and smiled as she dug through a couple of large boxes.

"Breaking and entering is still a crime around here, you know?" he said, causing her to jerk around. When she did so, she jumped up and bumped her head on a low shelf holding a box of papers, sending them showering over her.

He held in a chuckle as he rushed over to help her pick up the mess.

"You scared me," she exclaimed.

"Sorry," he mumbled as he knelt beside her.

"Your mother said I could stop by and see if there was anything else in here that I could use," she explained as she helped pick up the papers and books. Then her eyes moved past the papers and landed on him, and she frowned, then smiled slowly. "Did you spend your day making mud pies?" she joked.

He glanced down and realized every inch of him was caked in mud.

Groaning, he shook his head. "Helping someone get their truck out of the mud."

"Right," she said slowly, as if to give him the idea that she didn't believe him.

He finished putting the last of the books into the box

and replaced the box on the shelf. "Find anything you might want?" he asked. When her eyes ran over him and she sucked her bottom lip in between her teeth, he felt his body react.

"A few things," she answered finally.

His eyebrows rose as he thought about taking her, here, with the smell of fresh hay mixing with the soft scent of her perfume.

"I just don't know how I'm going to get it all over to the cottage," she added.

He glanced around. "Where's your truck?"

"Robin has it. She went to Portland to help my folks hold a garage sale. They're getting ready to sell their place and have a ton of stuff they wanted to get rid of. My sister, being the businessperson that she is, wanted to take over the entire process."

"How'd you get here?" he asked.

"Walked," she answered with a shrug.

He thought about the trip from the cottage to his parents' place and realized it was less than a few miles down the road. Even less if you went the beach route.

"You need your own car," he suggested.

"Why? It would only sit most of the time. Besides, I like walking."

"What are you going to do when it starts snowing?" he asked, remembering he'd asked her that the other day.

She shrugged and smiled. "Put on boots and a coat."

He sighed and shook his head. "I've got a truck."

Her eyes ran over him and then she laughed. "There is no way I'm letting you step foot in the cottage like that."

He glanced down again and groaned. "Yeah, as it is, I'm going to have to strip naked on the back doorstep just to get inside the house to shower off. My mother would kill me if I dropped so much as a clump of dirt on her floor."

Kara's laughter warmed him and, at the same time, further ignited his desires.

"If you want, I can head in and shower and then help you move over what you want?" he offered.

"I'll take you up on that offer," she said easily. "I found a cute coffee table." She motioned to the pile of furniture. "Somewhere in here. What is your mother going to do with all this? Open her own store?"

He chuckled. "She used to run an antique store. I think she still thinks she does sometimes." He shook his head. "I think my crib is still in here somewhere," he joked.

Kara laughed again. "I'll keep looking. You go clean up."

Conner walked in the back door of the house, stripped down to nothing more than his boxer briefs and socks, and avoided talking to his mother until he was done showering and dressing.

"So," he said, stepping into her art studio. She was sitting in front of the large bay windows, working on a large canvas. Her father was sitting in the corner, reading a book with the two dogs curled around his feet. "For years you've stockpiled furniture in that barn and now you're just giving it away?" he asked her.

His mother glanced over at him. A strand of her hair fell loose and slipped into her eyes, which she quickly wiped away with the back of her hand, spreading a dark blue streak of paint over her cheek as she did so.

He smiled and walked over to wipe it away with a cloth she kept nearby.

"I'm not giving it away," she said, turning back to her canvas.

"Don't tell me that you're making her pay for all that

junk?" He glanced out the windows towards the barn and could still see the light on out there.

"No, of course not." His mother turned to look at him with a smile. "We've come up with a deal. A trade of sorts."

His eyes narrowed. "A trade of what?"

"Well, she can have whatever she finds in the barn and I get one free event at her venue."

"That's not really fair."

His mother waved her paintbrush at him. "Sure, it is. I've been wanting to host a local art fair. It's not a large event and, really, no big planning on Kara's part." She turned back to the canvas. "Besides, it was her idea."

"Right," he said to her back. He turned to sign to his dad. "Did you know about this?"

His father shrugged and replied. "I learned a long time ago to stay out of your mother's business."

Conner chuckled. "Smart man," he signed back. "How did you expect her to get all that stuff back to her place?" he asked his mother.

"I knew you'd be along to help out soon enough," she threw over her shoulder. "Remember"—she glanced over her shoulder and wiped at the loose hair again, sending more color onto her cheeks and forehead—"lift with your legs not your back." She smiled.

"Meddler," he mumbled as he walked out. He heard his mother laugh as he headed out to help Kara move furniture. He'd walked right into his mother's trap. She knew that he had Wednesdays and Thursdays off. Had she requested Kara to stop by tonight knowing he didn't have to be anywhere early in the morning?

Shit. Did he even have protection still in his wallet? Would he need any? What was he thinking? He wasn't even sure Kara wanted him like that. Sure, they'd kissed a few times, but that didn't mean that she wanted to sleep with him.

He was getting way ahead of himself. Shaking off the thoughts of his mother trying to hook him up, he backed the truck up to the barn door and got to work helping Kara load up everything she'd picked out all while trying to keep the thought of her naked under him out of his mind.

"Everything okay?" she asked after the last of what she wanted had been loaded up in the back of his truck and they were on the road driving to the cottage.

"Yeah." He glanced over at her. "Just... tired," he lied.

"I'm sorry that I'm dragging you out again," Kara said.

"It's no bother. I wanted to help out." He backed up to get as close to the front door of the cottage as possible. Glancing over at her, he took a moment to appreciate just how perfect she was before jumping out and rushing around to open her door.

"You keep doing that," she said as he helped her down out of the truck.

"Another thing that, if I don't do it, I'm afraid my mother will find out," he joked.

"I had a lovely visit with your mother last Sunday. She hardly seemed like the scary type," she said, looking up at him.

He chuckled. "You're not family," he warned. He motioned to the full truck. "She told me about your deal."

Kara glanced over at the truck. "I think I got the better end of the bargain."

He shook his head. "For a few things? You probably charge more for the church group that meets there every week."

"And some of this furniture is worth double that. Your

mother knows that. You did say she used to own an antique store, correct?" Kara countered.

He shrugged. "It's your time," he admitted. "We'd better get moving." He nodded to the dark sky. "It feels like it's going to rain soon."

It took them less time to unload the items into the cottage than it had getting them out of the barn and putting them into the truck.

In the end, she'd picked out a coffee table, two end tables for the living room, a small table and chairs that she put in her sister's room, along with some outdoor furniture that used to be on their back porch. They had just set it up on the deck off the back of the cottage when the rain started.

"Thanks again for all your help tonight," she said over the thunder that shook the small cottage. The lights flashed and she jumped. Then everything went dark.

"Conner?" she asked as he pulled out her phone and turned the flashlight on.

"Easy," he said softly. "I'll go check the fuse box."

"I'll go with you." Kara's tone told him that she was worried and extremely afraid.

"Sure." He took her hand in his. She gripped his arm tightly and followed him into the kitchen.

"Where's the fuse box?" he asked after realizing he didn't know where he was going.

She shook her head. "I don't know."

"Okay, so we look." He turned the flashlight and looked all around the kitchen. He opened the pantry door and saw the fuse box at the back. "It's in here." He flipped the main circuit several times. "It looks like the main power is out." He glanced towards the windows. "It's probably out all over town." Her hand was back in his.

"What do you say we head in and sit down until the majority of the storm passes?" he suggested.

He felt her relax slightly. "Oh, okay. How about some tea? The stove is gas. There are candles in the drawer there." She pointed in the beam of the light to a drawer.

"I'll get them, you sit down. I'll make the tea." He nudged her into the chair and handed his cell phone to her. "Give me some light?"

She nodded, but before she had time to respond, he leaned in and kissed her.

CHAPTER ELEVEN

Kara couldn't stop the shaking. She knew it was childish to be afraid of a little lightning and thunder. For as long as she could remember, she'd frozen up each time the sky turned dark and angry.

Still, she tried to hold still while Conner fumbled around her kitchen and made them tea. Each time there was a loud crack, she jumped, sending the flashlight from his cell phone bouncing around the room.

"I have some cookies in the pantry," she suggested after he set the cups of tea down in front of her.

He nodded and then took the phone from her and used the light to hunt through her pantry for the cookies.

This time when he came back, he sat next to her.

"Are you doing okay?" he asked softly.

"Yeah." She tried to chuckle, but it came out as a nervous giggle instead. She felt her face heat and tried to avoid his eyes at her stupidity. She was thankful for the darkness as they drank their tea and snacked on the Milanos.

Thankfully, he started asking her about the upcoming events and, the shocker was, he actually listened to her ramble on about the coming parties she was planning.

She understood that most men would find what she did boring. Men enjoyed a good party, but most didn't want to hear or think about what went on behind the scenes.

It was nice when Conner asked her questions and seemed to enjoy hearing about her business. After a few minutes talking about it, she had completely relaxed, her mind off the storm outside and instead focused on just enjoying talking to the man sitting across from her.

"We finished off the entire bag of cookies," she said, waving the empty container. "I'll have to stop off and buy more in the morning before Robin gets back home."

For some reason, her comment had Conner standing up quickly and taking their empty mugs to the sink.

He was standing in the shadows now and it was too dark to see his expression, but she wagered he was uncomfortable leaving her there alone, in the dark.

Standing, she glanced out the window. The storm had died down, but the rain was still a steady stream outside the windows.

"I'll be okay here, by myself," she told him. "I didn't mean to keep you so long." She remembered him saying that he was tired earlier and figured that it was easily past ten o'clock at this point.

"Will you?" he asked from his spot in front of the sink.

She moved closer, trying to get a better look at his face so she could assess his mood.

"Thank you." She touched his shoulder. "For helping me out again."

He turned slightly and, in the candlelight, she could just make out his eyes, which were moving over her face.

"I really want to kiss you again," he said softly as he reached up and brushed her hair away from her face.

Immediately, she felt her knees weaken at the thought of kissing him again. Her body swayed towards his as her hands moved on their own accord to circle around his neck and pull him down until they were a breath away.

"Kara," he whispered as he brushed his lips over hers.

"Please," she sighed just before he took the kiss deeper.

She lost herself in the feeling of him as her hands roamed over his arms, his strong shoulders. Then she finally buried them in his thick hair, holding him to her as the kiss turned her entire body to jelly.

Without her knowing, he'd switched their positions until she was backed up against the countertop. His hands roamed over her body, causing a low moan of appreciation to escape her lips as he kissed her.

Then he was lifting her by the hips, setting her on the edge of the counter as he settled in between her thighs. She immediately wrapped her legs around him, pulling him closer against her core, where she wanted him.

She'd forgotten how wonderful it felt to be kissed, touched, pleased. His name escaped her lips as he started trailing his mouth down her neck, raising bumps all over her skin.

"Kara," he groaned as he pulled off the sweatshirt she'd put on when she'd walked over to the Jordan's place. His eyes roamed over the almost see-through white tank top she wore underneath.

She felt her nipples pucker under his watchful eye and heard his groan of appreciation. Then his hand slowly moved up her ribs until he cupped her.

"Perfect," he said softly. The feeling of him touching

her had her rolling her head back and closing her eyes on a moan as her legs jerked around him.

"Conner, I don't think I can wait," she said as she reached to remove his shirt.

He let her tug it over his head and toss it onto the counter next to them.

A slow smile spread on her lips as she ran her eyes over the lean muscle's underneath. She had appreciated the view of his bare chest in the moonlight when he'd pulled her from the water, but now, in the glowing light of the candles, she could see even more of him.

The light danced over his toned, tanned skin like an exotic dance. Reaching up, she trailed her fingertips over his pecs as she bit her bottom lip.

"Keep looking at me like that and you may get your wish not to wait too long." He hoisted her up into his arms as she locked her ankles behind his back. She held onto him as he started walking towards her bedroom door.

For a split second, she worried how she'd left her room that morning, but then he bent his head down and kissed her and she forgot everything but him.

Since they'd left the burning candles on the table, when he shut the bedroom door behind them, they were shrouded in darkness.

"Damn," he groaned. "Guess I should've grabbed a candle."

She chuckled nervously. "I could—"

"No, just point me in the direction of the bed."

"It's straight ahead, about five feet."

He moved slowly until his leg hit the edge of the mattress. Then he sighed and shifted to lay her down.

"I'll be right back. I want to be able to see you." Her

bedroom door opened and a moment later he returned holding one of the candles and their discarded clothes. "I didn't think you'd want your sister to find our clothes there, if she comes back early."

She smiled, just knowing that he planned on spending the entire night there, with her.

She nervously waited and watched as he set the candle down on her nightstand and then turned back towards her. His eyes moved over her slowly.

"I'm thankful the lights went out," he said softly. "You look amazing in candlelight." He settled on the edge of her bed and reached for her.

Getting up on her knees, she moved over to wrap her arms around his shoulders and pull him across the bed to kiss her. When her body bumped up against his, she felt his desire against her stomach and was thankful he was holding her steady.

"Easy," he said softly against her lips. "I've got you."

"Conner, I..." She shook her head. "It's been... a while," she admitted, feeling like a fool.

"For me as well," he said, running his hands slowly over her. He nudged the tank top higher as his fingertips traced over her lower ribs. "God, I want you." He bent down to place a kiss on her shoulder.

She leaned back as he gently pulled off the rest of her clothes, leaving her kneeling on the bed in her cotton bra and the little strip of matching cotton underwear.

"If I'd known this is how the night would end, I would have worn silk," she said nervously.

"It's perfect. You're perfect." He traced the material with a fingertip.

Once again, her nipples peaked at his slight touch.

When she reached for the snap of his jeans, he pulled back and quickly kicked his jeans aside, returning to her in only his boxer briefs.

When he kissed her this time, he nudged her backward until she was tucked under him on the mattress. His hands moving over her had her purring and moving under him, trying to get him to go faster. She wanted him. Needed him.

"Please," she cried out when he moved her panties aside and ran a finger over her.

She heard and felt him chuckle, his chest vibrating against her own.

She cried out his name when he dipped a finger into her.

"My god," he said against her skin. She cried out when his weight disappeared from her. She tried to reach out and hold him to her, but he chuckled again.

"Easy, I'm right here." He reappeared lower, trailing his mouth over her belly. He dipped his tongue into her belly button as his fingers continued to please her. When his mouth covered her pussy, she arched up and felt herself explode against his tongue.

"My god," he said again as he moved up and covered her. She realized he'd removed the last barriers between them and heard him ripping open a condom package before settling between her legs. "You taste like nectar," he said, leaning in and running his mouth over her neck.

Her hands reached around him as she gripped his hips. She felt her entire body pulsing as he shifted over her. How had he built her up again so soon? It was as if he'd just warmed her up and now, now, she needed him beyond everything else.

"Please, Conner, I..." She dug her fingernails into his hips. "Don't make me wait."

"No." He smiled down at her. "No more waiting." He slid slowly into her and started moving, building her up again. She moved with him, running her fingernails over his skin as she held onto him and he pleased her.

This time, when she felt herself fall, she knew Conner was right there with her. He cried out her name as he tensed inside her.

When his body went lax over hers, she held onto him as their breathing settled together.

"I'll move," he groaned a moment later.

"No, don't," she begged.

Just then, they both jumped slightly when her bedroom light flashed on. The room was so bright, she had to blink a few times. She'd been bathed in soft candlelight moments before, but now her naked body was exposed in the bright light, and she reached for the blankets.

"I'll shut it off," Conner said, rolling off her.

As much as she wanted to cover herself and hide from him, she was thankful he felt confident enough to walk across her bedroom stark naked. As muscular as his chest and arms were, his thighs and ass were just as impressive.

When he flipped the light switch, she held in a groan and wished instantly for a little longer assessment of him.

Then he was back in the bed with her and tucking her into his arms.

"Sleep for a while," he mumbled. "Then I know I'll want you again." He kissed her cheek.

She shifted in his hold slightly and trailed her mouth over his neck in return.

"Kara." His tone was low, like a warning.

She smiled. "What if I don't want to wait?" She shifted until she lay over him as she continued to rub her body against his slowly.

She smiled even more when she felt him grow hard again.

"You're going to be the death of me," he said, then he quickly flipped her and settled between her thighs again.

CHAPTER TWELVE

Conner woke with Kara's hair in his face and her bare breasts pushed against his chest, and he smiled. Her scent had filled his dreams while her softness had been pushed up against his body all night.

He couldn't remember having a more wonderful night's sleep before. His hands started slowly moving over her soft hip as he felt his body waking quickly.

When she moaned and shifted slightly in his arms, he knew she was just as affected as he was.

"Conner," she moaned softly when he slipped into her.

"Morning," he chuckled as he snuggled into her hair, trailing his mouth over her neck. "God, I love the smell of you in the morning," he sighed as he moved with her.

He loved the feeling of her legs wrapped around him, the way she held onto him. The little sexy sounds she made when she came, which caused him to follow her. Breathing heavily, he collapsed and held on as their heartbeats slowed together.

"What time will your sister be back?" he asked moments later.

She shifted and looked over at him. "Around nine."

He glanced at his phone and winced. "Guess that means we won't get to enjoy breakfast together."

She rolled over until she rested her head in her hands, propped up on her elbow. "We could head into town and grab something at Sara's Nook?"

He smiled. "Now that's a plan." He rolled out of bed and started dressing quickly.

"I'll meet you there," she said crawling out of bed. "I need a shower."

"I'll head home and change and then swing by to pick you up." He leaned over and kissed her as she sat on the edge of the bed, holding the blankets to her naked body. "Half an hour," he warned and then quickly left after she nodded.

He stepped outside directly into a shroud of mist and fog. He'd grown up with countless mornings along the Oregon coast that were filled with whiteout conditions such as this. Still, driving back to his place, he used extra caution since he knew school buses and kids walking to school were out and about at this time of the morning.

Parking behind his dad's truck, he let himself in the back door and snuck into his bathroom to shower and change.

He hoped to avoid running into either of his parents or his brother but knew that the chances were slim.

When he stepped out of the hallway to head back out, he bumped into Jacob, who was dressed and ready for work.

"Could use your help today," Jacob signed. It was an old habit of theirs, signing when they knew their mother could still be asleep.

"Can't, have plans," he signed back, and headed down

the stairs. Jacob followed him and, when they reached the kitchen, stopped him again.

"What kind of plans?" Jacob asked.

"I'm helping a friend out," he replied as he put on his shoes by the back door while Jacob grabbed a glass of orange juice.

"Listen, I don't ask for much, but Rose has me in a bind. I could use some solidarity." Jacob glanced over at him.

Conner shrugged. "You know, you two have never gotten along." Then he had a thought and a burst of laughter exploded from him. "And to think that I used to believe Rose had a secret crush on you." He shook his head as he left out the back door. Had he seen his brother's face pale slightly?

When he pulled up in front of the cottage, the old truck that Kara shared with her sister was sitting out front. He winced when he realized he hadn't gotten Kara's cell number from her yet so he could text her that he was there.

Just as he was about to climb out of the truck to head up and knock on the door, a dark figure emerged from the home.

When Kara climbed into the truck, he held out his phone. "Program your number for me?" he asked. "I meant to get it the other day."

Her smile doubled and she nodded as she took the phone.

After she handed it back to him, he shot off a message to her and waited until her phone chimed.

"There, now we can talk anytime. Day or night." He sighed and took her hand in his, then kissed it.

"Does that mean it's official?" she asked.

His eyebrows shot up as he backed up. "I would think that after last night..."

"I'm joking." She nudged him on the shoulder.

He chuckled. "Just so we're clear."

"We are." She smiled over at him, and he felt his heart skip a beat.

Sitting in the bakery with Kara while the people of Pride came and went, he figured it was also obvious to anyone who saw them sitting next to one another in the booth. His arm was wrapped around Kara's shoulder as they sipped their coffee and had sugary pastries.

She filled him in on her sister's visit with their parents. Their folks were getting ready to sell their home in Portland.

"They're hoping to purchase a place closer to Pride," she said as she finished the last bite of a breakfast quiche. "Since we're both determined to remain here."

He thought about his own future. At one point a few years back, he'd been determined to leave Pride. Two years in the city for school had quickly changed his mind, and he'd returned home.

Then again, he hadn't done anything to make the return more permanent. In fact, he was still living in his childhood bedroom, under his parents' roof. Sure, he had an excellent job, but most guys in his position had their own places or lived in the barracks. He'd thought about finding his own place and now that he was looking forward to a relationship with Kara, the need to do so had grown.

"Have they had any luck finding a place?" he asked, curious to see what was available.

"I think they've found a rental until the new subdivision your family is working on opens up." Kara shrugged.

Damn, why hadn't he thought of that himself? He knew that they were scheduled to start building the new homes in two short months. He could be on the list of first home buyers if he wanted.

"Good idea," he said under his breath.

"What?" She arched her eyebrows and looked over at him.

Shaking his head, he sighed. "I've been thinking the same."

"Oh?" She turned slightly towards him. "Is that why you're avoiding working with Jacob?"

He nudged her. "Trust me, if you'd witnessed him and Rose bickering, you'd avoid them too."

"I saw them the other day at the hardware store." Kara nodded. "I see what you mean. They were arguing over what type of flags to buy. You know, the kind you put out to mark property lines."

"Right. They went with pink. They're everywhere up there now." He motioned towards the hill overlooking the town.

Kara's eyes followed his gaze. "It's hard to believe that soon there will be homes up there."

"One hundred and thirty to start with."

"Wow, that many?"

"Plus a clubhouse, state-of-the-art gym, pool, tennis courts, and more."

"Wow, I'm going to have to head up there and take a look at it all for myself."

"Right now, it's just a bunch of dirt being moved around." He took her hand and realized he'd taken enough of her time that morning. She probably had work to get to. Besides, he wanted to do a little home searching himself before dinner tonight.

"What are your plans now?" she asked out of the blue.

He shrugged, not wanting to tell her he was probably

going to spend the day looking for a place to live and talk to his brother about setting a lot aside for him.

"I'm free," she suggested. "Why don't you take me up there so I can see it for myself? That way, I can get some information for my folks."

"Are you sure?" he asked her.

She chuckled and nudged his shoulder. "What does a girl have to do to get you to spend the day with her? Beg?"

"You don't have work?"

She slowly shook her head. "Not until tomorrow."

He shrugged. "Okay, I'm game. You may want to change into some boots." He helped her out of the booth. "And maybe some old jeans." He glanced down at his own tennis shoes. "I'll need to change too."

"You can drop me off and then stop by on the way out of town to pick me up." She started to pull some cash out of her purse.

He stopped her and quickly paid for their breakfast.

"Okay," she said as her eyes narrowed, "but I'm buying next time."

He shrugged. "It's up to you."

She got up on her toes and kissed him. "It's what I want."

He smiled, knowing that they had been standing in full view of the large window at the bakery. No doubt, the entire town would know about them by the end of the day. For some reason, that fact pleased him immensely.

He walked into his parents' house, and his mother caught him just as he was climbing the stairs to change into his work jeans and boots.

"Your brother told me that you were sneaking out of here early?" she asked, holding a large bucket of laundry that no doubt held some of his clothes. He'd tried to convince her when he moved back in that he was capable of taking care of himself, but so far she hadn't allowed him to lift a finger around the place except to move furniture or make repairs.

"Yeah." He took the basket from her. "I'll take these upstairs. I'm going to be heading out to the site after I change."

He saw the surprise in her eyes at this news. "Jacob said you were too busy today helping a friend?"

"Plans changed," he called over his shoulder as he headed up the stairs.

When he came back down, his parents were gone, most likely out on a walk since both dogs were MIA as well.

When he drove back over to the cottage, he knew it was past time to move out. He'd pretty much talked himself into finding the first rental place that was available.

He drove through town and slammed on his brakes when he saw the sign above O'Neil's grocery store.

Why hadn't he thought of the apartment before now? Pulling into the small parking lot, he rushed in and, ten minutes later, walked out of the store with a smile on his face and a set of keys to his new place in his pockets.

"You look happy," Kara said as she climbed into his truck.

"I'm moving," he blurted out.

Her smile slipped and turned into a frown.

"You are? Where to?"

"The apartment above O'Neil's." He saw her relax.

"I drove by after she put out the sign. Apparently, she's had the place empty while Parker was doing some renovations. The place is ready, and I'll be moving in tomorrow." He frowned suddenly. "Well, tomorrow after work."

"That's great news. I didn't know you were officially

looking for a place of your own," she said as he pulled onto the main road that would take them up the hill towards the new subdivision.

"I wasn't really, but I figured after last night..." He reached over and took her hand. "I'd like some privacy with you."

"Good idea," she said with a sigh. "I was wondering what I was going to tell Robin. Not that I don't love living with my sister in a little cottage, but it would be nice to have some time with you without making her feel..."

"Like a third wheel?" he said, and she nodded in agreement.

"So, tell me about this subdivision," she said, and he chuckled when she pulled a notepad from her purse to take notes.

"Hidden Cove," he supplied. "Homes will range from eighteen hundred square feet to just above three-thousand. Two- or three-car garages. Each lot will be three quarters of an acre."

"Wow, that sounds just up my parents' alley," she broke in after writing down some notes. "Dad likes his toys." She glanced over at him. "My mother swears she needs a four-car garage just to keep his riding lawn mower, motorcycles, and other gadgets in."

"I think I'm going to like your dad," he joked. "My dad has an entire barn. But in the past few years, my mother has filled it with stuff. She remodeled the entire inside of their home a few years back and instead of selling off stuff..."

"Yeah, I know, she gives it away to strangers," Kara said with a chuckle.

"Right." He rolled his eyes and turned off the main road to head up the long private road. "This will be the main entrance. There will be a gate here." He slowed the truck down. "A grand stone entrance with a sign. Rose has the drawings all done. I'll show it to you when we get up to the construction trailer." He continued up the steep drive and parked beside his brother's truck.

"We'll head inside first and grab a map of the lots before hiking around so I can show you where everything will be."

He opened the door to the trailer and then stood in shock as his eyes adjusted to the scene of Jacob and Rose in each other's arms in a heated embrace.

CHAPTER THIRTEEN

When Conner slammed the trailer door shut, Kara grew concerned, until he turned towards her and shook his head.

"I knew it." He chuckled, then glanced around and knocked his boots a couple times on the small steps. He opened the door again, more slowly this time.

When Kara stepped into the trailer, Conner was sitting behind the desk, looking down at a computer screen and Rose, a woman roughly Kara's age, whom she hadn't officially met yet, was standing a few feet away looking down at her phone.

When Kara took in the blush on Rose's cheeks and noticed the woman's long dark hair coming free from a French braid, she guessed that the pair had either been in a fight or had been doing something else moments before.

It was very obvious to Kara that the two were embarrassed about something, and she glanced towards Conner, who was just smiling like a loon.

"Hey," he said to his brother. "Kara's folks are looking to move to Pride, and she wants some information on what's available."

"Oh," Rose jumped in. "How wonderful." She held out her hand. "I'm Rose Derby."

"Kara Jenkins." She shook the pretty brunette's hand. "Why don't you come back here to my office. I'll show you the plans we have so far." She motioned for Kara to follow her into the other small office.

"So, what's new?" Kara heard Conner say just before Rose shut the door between them.

The woman looked relieved to be out of the room.

"Is everything okay?" Kara asked, innocently.

"Yes." Rose sighed. "Just..." She shook her head quickly. "Yes." She smiled. "Why don't you tell me what your parents are looking for."

A few minutes later, Conner walked in and they spent the next half hour going over every floor plan Rose had designed for the subdivision.

Kara liked a few of them and snapped pictures to text to her folks.

Then they were shown a large map of the subdivision, which had all the lots and roads mapped out on it.

"Phase one will start in a few weeks, after they are done cutting and completing the roads. Sewage and electric are going in now, so if you show her around today, be careful. There are a lot of workers out there."

"Will do." Conner nodded. "I'm planning to build here myself."

Rose's eyebrows shot up. "You are?"

He chuckled. "Yeah. I just signed a lease on the apartment above O'Neil's, so I have plenty of time."

"That's wonderful," Rose said easily. "I don't know what I would do if I didn't have the option of staying at my parents' place." Rose turned to Kara. "My folks purchased a summer home near here shortly before I was born. We used to spend each summer down here."

"We did too. Well, a few weeks each summer when my parents could get away from work. Only my folks never purchased a place. We'd always stay at the bed and breakfast."

"You did?" Rose asked. "I bet we ran into one another plenty of times over the years. Either at the beach or somewhere in town."

"Probably." Kara nodded in agreement.

"Well, anyway, here's a smaller copy of this map so you can go out and look at which lots are available. Some of them have higher prices due to the views." She motioned to a row of squares on the map. "These all have great views of the beach below. We'll have a private access pathway and stairs leading down the cliff to the beach below here." She motioned to a spot. "Only ten sites will have those views."

"Nine," Conner corrected. "I've snagged this one for myself." He motioned to the last lot, which sat off on its own at the end of the street.

"You did?" Rose asked.

"Just made the deal with my uncle over the phone and cleared it with the foreman." Conner motioned to the other room. "Jacob thinks I'm crazy to let you design my home. I told him I was crazy to let him build it," he added with a smile.

Rose touched his arm. "Thank you. You're our first official sale. Well, if you don't count your cousins' homes that we're building on the adjoining property." She turned back to Kara. "We haven't officially opened up any lots for sale yet. Your parents will have plenty of time to decide which lot and home design they want. We hoped to start letting people in once the main roads are finished in about a month."

"The perks of being related to the developer," Jacob said from the doorway.

"You know, Robin and I had talked about building a bigger house on the land that came with the cottage and the barn," Kara admitted.

"If you get to the point that you want to start designing a place, let me know," Rose said quickly.

For the next half hour, Conner looked over all the house plans. Kara had to admit, she'd narrowed it down to two styles she really liked for her parents and one she dreamed of for herself. It surprised her a little that Conner quickly chose that one for the land he'd picked out.

"That's the floorplan I had hoped someone would pick for the lot you picked out," Rose said with a little sigh. "It's my favorite." She smiled at him. "Perfect for someone who plans on having a large family." Rose's eyes moved over to Kara's. Then it was her turn to flush as she avoided the woman's eyes.

Did Conner want a large family? What was she even thinking? Sure, they'd had one wonderful night together, but as far as she knew, he wasn't even thinking of commitments yet. Was he? It was far too soon to think of anything beyond that day. She tried to convince herself of that as they headed out to look at the lots at the top of the hill where his plot of land was.

She liked a few lots for her parents and figured that since they were moving to their retirement home, they would want to overlook the water themselves.

"You got quiet," Conner said after parking his truck in the dirt along the side of what would be the road soon.

"Just trying to imagine how all of this will look," she lied.

"I can't believe little Rose has the skills to create those wonderful home plans," he said with a chuckle as he helped her out of the truck.

She was thankful she'd changed into her hiking boots and worn jeans, as her feet sank a little in the mud.

Conner didn't seem to mind or care that they had to walk through the muck that last night's rain had caused. He held onto her hand and helped her through the worst of it as they made their way to where little signs showed them where each lot was.

"This one's mine." He motioned to the small sign. "We'll have to walk through the brush to see the view. They won't clear the lot until after the roads are in."

As they made their way through the thick bushes, Conner held back the branches to let her pass. She avoided a few spiderwebs and would have stepped directly in one if Conner hadn't stopped her and used a stick to knock the massive thing down.

She pulled the hood of her hoodie up and tightened it, afraid of getting webs or spiders in her hair. She shivered visibly each time that she noticed a web sparkling in the daylight. Even though she had to admit that some of them were beautiful, she still cringed each time she noticed the massive things.

"I swear I'm not usually this squeamish," she told Conner after he'd knocked down a few more webs with a stick.

He chuckled. "My mother and sister are the same way." He turned to her and laughed when she tightened the hoodie of her sweatshirt even more. "You know, they don't set out to climb on people. Think about it, we're what? A million times bigger than they are. Imagine seeing a creature that large hovering over you. You'd run the other way as fast as possible."

"Yeah, but I don't have eight legs and drink blood." She shivered visibly, causing him to laugh even more.

"Fair point." He motioned to the clearing ahead of them.

When they stepped out of the thickest part of the bushes, the view opened up and she gasped at the beauty.

"Wow." She tried to take in everything. The beautiful Oregon coastline lay beyond a small grassy hill. A little over a hundred yards below them sat a pristine beach with dark rocks jutting out of the blue Pacific waters while white waves crashed along the sandy beach. Down the other way, the lighthouse sat, a white column in the midst of the grassy hillside along the shoreline.

"The property line is here," Conner said, motioning to a little pink flag that sat halfway across the green hill. "The house will sit up there." He turned and motioned to the thick trees. "Once it's cleared of most of the trees. I'll want to keep a lot of the bigger ones." He tilted his head as if imagining it all. "Maybe Rose can add more windows off the back of the place." He turned back to the view as he smiled slowly. "I'll build a large deck." He glanced from side to side. "I'll add some stairs down to the beach just past a nice wide yard."

She listened to him dream about his future home and could actually see everything he was talking about. Her heart ached at the thought of having her own future so planned out. So... perfect.

Then Conner turned to her and shook his head. "Sorry, I didn't mean to hijack your time. We're supposed to be looking for your parents."

"It's okay," she said, avoiding his eyes. "It's so peaceful up here. I've pretty much made up my mind that they should have one of the lots looking out over the water. I'm positive they're going to want to see this every day."

He walked over and wrapped his arm around her. "My folks' place has a beautiful view, but somehow from up this high it's just..." She felt him shrug his shoulders behind her as his other arm wrapped around her. Now her back was to his chest, and he rested his chin on the top of her head. "It's perfect," he finished with a sigh.

He was right. There, standing with his arms wrapped around her, everything did feel perfect.

She closed her eyes for a moment and tried to hold onto the daydream that he'd built up in her mind as he'd talked.

"Come on. We can take the cleared path to the other lots." He motioned to the left. "You can take pictures of the view and the lots for your parents."

When he dropped his arms from her, she swayed a little and held in a shiver as a cool breeze washed over her. Wrapping her arms around herself, she followed him towards the other lots and decided the last one they walked by was the one for her parents. It was at the base of the hill so that her parents would be able to walk out their back door and head down a small grassy hill to get to the beach.

Conner stood by as she took more than a dozen pictures of the view and the land. They walked back towards where the road would be, and she realized that there were fewer trees on this lot.

They spent a few hours there, looking at the house plans and then walking the land. By the time they headed back to his truck, a light mist had covered the area and it was beginning to rain again.

Since they'd left his truck up near his lot, they climbed

the low sloped hill to where he'd parked. Just then a truck turned the corner and flew down the muddy roadway, heading directly towards them. Its bright headlights blinded them momentarily.

Immediately, Conner pulled her further off the roadway and when large clumps of dirt started to hit them, Conner cursed and tried to shield her with his body. She cried out as a clump of dirt or maybe a large rock hit her in the calf, causing pain to explode and her legs to buckle beneath her.

CHAPTER FOURTEEN

"You didn't see who it was?" Jacob asked for the second time.

"No." Conner ran his hands through his wet hair and cursed under his breath as Rose helped roll up Kara's jeans to look at the large red mark on her calf.

"If it was one of my guys, I'll find out. I won't tolerate this kind of recklessness on my job site," Jacob said sternly.

When she'd cried out and buckled in his arms, he'd been so concerned about her that he hadn't looked at the truck. Instead, he'd raced up the hill towards his truck with Kara in his arms.

"I should have looked at the truck, but when it was heading towards us, it had its high beams on and, well, I didn't have time to do anything except make sure we weren't in its direct path," he admitted. "How is she?" he asked Rose.

"I'm fine," Kara answered. "As I said many times before." She touched his arms. "Really, it was just dirt."

"By the look of this, dirt with a few rocks in it," Rose added, looking down at Kara's red skin.

"Okay, yeah, there had to be a few rocks," Kara admitted with a hiss when Rose ran her fingers over the back of her calf.

Kara was trying to twist and get a better look at the back of her leg. She winced when she noticed her marred skin.

"I should take you to see my uncle." He reached to pick her up, but she stopped him.

"Conner, it was dirt and rocks. I've had worse. I can still walk. Nothing is broken. I'm not bleeding."

"I'd put some ice on it and keep it elevated for the rest of the day," Rose suggested. "It is pretty swollen."

"Good idea," Kara said, then she glanced at him.

He swallowed his concern, knowing it wasn't doing her or him any good.

"I'll take you home," he said, feeling a little defeated that their day had been cut short. He moved to pick her up again, only to have her nudge him aside and stand on her own.

"I can walk," she assured him with a smile as she tugged her jean leg back into place.

He held onto her as she limped towards the door.

"Thanks," Kara said to Rose. "Oh, hold lot seven for my parents. I'll see if they can come down next weekend to look at it themselves."

"Will do," Rose said with a smile. "I look forward to meeting them. Take care of your leg. We'll see you around."

"Thanks," Kara said again.

The moment they were outside, he lifted her into his arms and carried her the rest of the way to his truck.

"I could have walked," Kara said.

"I like carrying you," he answered as he set her down in the truck.

"Who do you think that was?" she asked as they started making their way down the hill. "A worker?"

"No," he answered after a moment. He had an idea of who it was but didn't want to involve her in his family's messy business.

"There's a rumor going around town about a developer that's giving your family problems," she said when they were driving slowly through town. "Do you think it could be him?"

"Yeah." He sighed. "Thomas Carson wanted the land. My uncle purchased all the land we were just on from an old friend of the family. Carson was rumored to be doing some..."—he shook his head as he remembered what everyone had gone through last year—"sinister activities to draw the land values down in the area so he could purchase the land cheap. My uncle purchased it all for market value and is looking at getting all the other land Mr. Carson wanted to get his hands on. He was going to develop a large resort."

He parked in front of her cottage. "I can't imagine a resort in Pride," she said with a shake of her head.

"Yeah, it would have ruined the town," he agreed.

She was quiet for a while as they waited for the rain to let up before they rushed into the cottage.

"What does this Thomas Carson look like?" she asked a moment later.

He shrugged. "I don't think I've ever seen him. Why?"

She sighed. "I... there was a man who stopped by last week in an awfully expensive suit. He claimed to be a lawyer, but..."

He turned towards her, suddenly flooded with concern. "What did he do?"

"Nothing, just... He said he represented a client who wanted to purchase our land," she said in a faint voice.

He thought about it. "My cousin knows what he looks like. I can call her and ask?"

"No, I'm sure it was nothing. I told the lawyer we weren't interested, and he left." She smiled over at him.

"If he comes around again, let me know." He felt a slight tightness in his chest.

She scanned his face and then nodded slowly. "I know I said I'd make you dinner, but..."

"I was thinking of ordering something for us from the Oar," he broke in, and relief flooded her face.

"That would be great. I didn't get a chance to head to the store and, well, I could use a nap," she added with a chuckle.

He smiled. "Go in, put some ice on your leg, and get some rest. I'm going to go run some errands. Then I'll pick us up dinner and see you back here at..."

"Six," she supplied.

He nodded. "Call in your order at the restaurant and then text me and I'll pick it up."

"Sounds wonderful," she said with a sigh. "I'm going to go in and show Robin the pictures of the land and show her the brochures for the houses. I'm sure she's going to agree that our folks should buy the place."

"I'll see you later," he promised, then leaned in and placed a soft kiss on her lips before she could climb out of the truck. He watched her limp towards the door and waited until she was inside before he backed up and headed towards his uncle's place.

He pulled into the small parking area at his uncle Todd's home. He dashed through the rain and let himself into the massive home.

Todd and Megan had always run a bed and breakfast out of their home. There were several cottages that they rented out between the main house and the beach. The front door was rarely locked and there was always a delicious meal and friendship waiting inside.

He found Todd and Megan in the kitchen, sitting at the table with his two-year-old twin nephew and niece, Ethan and Ellie.

The twins were both happily making a mess with their sandwiches and soup. His aunt and uncle appeared as if they were enjoying the entire fiasco instead of worried about the destruction of their kitchen by their oldest grandchildren.

Todd and Megan Jordan had been as steady in his childhood as his own parents had. There had been times when the lines of parenthood had blurred. It was as if he'd had three sets of parents between them, his aunt Lacey and Uncle Aaron, and his own parents. All of his cousins had felt the same and had even thought of themselves as siblings instead of cousins.

"Hey." His uncle chuckled upon seeing him. "We were just having some lunch. Grab a bowl of soup and help yourself to some grilled cheese sandwiches."

"Uncle Conner." Ellie clapped her chubby hands and held them for him.

He walked over and easily picked her up and sat down with her in his lap. She immediately began eating again and even reached up to give him a soggy piece of sandwich, which he ate.

Her long blonde hair was tied in two ponytails, which were coming out of their clips. Her brother Ethan was too busy eating to worry about the new visitor.

"What's on your mind?" Megan asked as she helped Ethan scoop up a spoonful of tomato soup.

"Thomas Carson," he said. His uncle jerked and stiffened.

"Is he bothering you?" Todd Jordan asked quickly.

"No, not me directly. I think he—" He stopped talking when Ellie shoved another soggy piece of bread in his mouth. He smiled at her and made sounds of pleasure, showing her that he was enjoying the food she was sharing with him. "I think he's paid Kara and her sister a visit. She mentioned some lawyer stopped by and informed her that his client wanted to put an offer on their land."

"And you think it's Carson?" Todd asked.

"It would stand to reason. Do you know anyone else interested in purchasing land around Pride who would send a lawyer in a suit?" he asked.

Todd sighed. "No. I'll see if Aiden can sniff around town and keep an eye out for someone who matches the description."

"While you're at it, you might want to have him keep an eye out for a blue four-by-four Ford truck. One with a bunch of mud on it."

Todd's eyebrows shot up. "Why?"

He glanced down at his niece and sighed. "The driver just bombarded Kara and I with mud pellets. She has a large welt on her leg to show for it."

"Oh no," Megan gasped. "Is she okay?"

"Yeah, she's at home resting. We were up at the land looking at the lots," he supplied.

"Todd texted me and told me that you've picked a lot out for yourself?" Megan asked.

He nodded. "Kara was looking for one for her parents who will be moving down from Portland soon."

"Alice and Eric are finally going to be moving here?" Megan asked with a smile.

Conner frowned. "You know Kara's folks?"

Megan laughed. "Of course. They've been coming her longer than any of our other guests. We've known the Jenkins family forever. Alice and Eric spent a few nights here one Christmas and got snowed in when you were just a baby. Then, after they married and had the girls, they started coming back each summer."

Conner shook his head and shifted Ellie on his lap. He should have known. Kara had told him she'd spent most of her summers here at his aunt's place. He just hadn't expected his aunt to remember every guest that had stayed in the cabins.

"Right." He nodded. "Yeah, she's trying to convince them to purchase a place in Hidden Cove."

"Oh, they're going to love it. I'm going to have to call Alice later tonight." Megan picked up Ethan, who was almost falling asleep in his soup bowl.

"I think these two need a bath and then a nap before Mom and Dad come pick them up in a few hours." She shifted Ethan to her hip and then gracefully leaning over to pick up Ellie and place her on her other hip. "There are fresh sandwiches and warm soup. Stay for lunch," Megan said before leaving the room with a baby on each hip.

He watched his aunt go, holding the two babies as if she'd done it a million times.

"She's good at that," he said unconsciously.

Todd chuckled. "There for a few years, we had so many kids running around this place, it was hard to remember which ones were our own."

Conner chuckled. "I was just thinking how wonderful it was growing up with three moms and dads." He sighed and reached for a fresh un-soggy sandwich as his uncle stood up and walked over to the fridge.

"Beer?" he asked over his shoulder.

"Yeah," he said after taking a bite of the sandwich. "I've got a few hours to kill before heading back over to Kara's for dinner. I was going to start moving some of my things over to the apartment."

His uncle popped the top on two beers and handed him one as his eyebrows shot up.

"Apartment?" Todd asked.

"Yeah, I convinced Patty to let me rent the place above the store," he answered with a slight shrug.

"Needing more privacy?" Todd joked.

"It's sort of hard to date when you are still living under your parents' roof." He sipped the beer.

"So, there is more to you helping Kara out?" Todd asked.

Conner thought about it. He'd never kept anything from his family before and wasn't going to start now. Not with something this important.

"Yeah," he said, and took a sip of the beer. "Yeah, there is."

CHAPTER FIFTEEN

———————————

Kara slept like the dead. The ice pack she'd placed on her calf had at some point slipped off her leg and landed on her bed, soaking the sheets. When she woke, almost two hours after Conner had dropped her off at the cottage, she was refreshed but sore. She tested her leg out and figured a hot shower might loosen the muscles in her calf.

Already there was a massive bruise and several small red marks where rocks must have hit her skin through her jeans. Her entire calf was double its usual size.

By the time she was dressed in gray leggings and a large cream-colored sweater with her hair curled and lying over her shoulders, she felt back to normal and almost sent Conner a text to let him know that she'd cook tonight. But then she remembered that Robin had told her that she needed to go into Edgeview for some supplies, so Kara would need to walk to the store to get groceries. One glance out the window confirmed that the rain hadn't let up since Conner had dropped her off.

Instead, she decided to spend her time baking. Since she had the supplies to make cookies, she got to work mixing the dough as she flipped on the television and listened to an old black-and-white movie. She danced to one of the songs playing on the set.

Her sister walked in just as she was taking the first batch of cookies out of the oven.

"Wow, those smell good," Robin said, reaching for one. "How's the leg?" she asked before taking a bite of the hot cookie. She'd texted her sister what had happened before lying down.

"Fine," Kara answered, then grabbed a cookie for herself. "A little sore, but nothing too bad." She wiggled her leg and tested it out. "Sore but in working order."

Robin chuckled. "We can call in our order to the Oar. After driving to pick up all the new chair and table covers, I'm starving. It took all my will not to hit the drive-through while I was in Edgeview."

"I have the menu pulled up on my iPad." She motioned to where she'd set her iPad earlier and turned to put another batch of cookies in the oven.

"Who is this?" Robin asked holding up her iPad. An image of Thomas Carson filled the screen.

"That's the man who stopped by last week and claimed he was a lawyer." Kara shut the oven and walked over to look at the image over her sister's shoulder. "He's the guy the Jordans are having issues with."

"The land shark?" Robin asked. Kara nodded.

"He stopped by here?" Her sister turned to her.

"Yeah, the night of the Johnson's anniversary party. I was heading over here to grab a new roll of double-sided tape and bumped into him on the pathway. He claimed he was a lawyer and had a client interested in making an offer for our place."

"He's not a lawyer?" Robin asked.

"No, he's a developer for C&C Investment. It says here he's preparing to start a large multi-million-dollar project along the Oregon coast that will draw thousands of investors."

"Sounds like one of those condo time-share scams," Robin said, looking over the website Kara had pulled up earlier.

"Yeah, except they are looking to bring in large investors, claiming the area is the next 'it' zone." Kara turned away and checked on the cookies. "I'll call in dinner. Conner should be ready to pick up the food soon."

"Sure." Her sister changed gears and looked over the menu for the restaurant and gave her order to her. "So, you and Conner?" she said as she scanned the list.

Kara couldn't stop the smile. "Yeah, it was very unexpected."

"But good, right?" Robin asked her as she looked over the iPad.

Kara felt her face heat and her smile double. "Yes, very."

Her sister sighed and went back to looking at the screen. "He has a brother, right?"

Kara chuckled. "Yes, but something tells me that Jacob is..." She thought about how the man had acted around Rose and chuckled. "Entangled."

Robin's eyebrows shot up and then she shrugged. "Probably just as well. I'm more into the intellectual type anyway."

Kara thought back to all of her sister's boyfriends and realized that she'd always dated the nerd types. Jacob Jordan was anything but nerdy. He was full brawn mountain man wrapped in a flannel package. As she washed dishes, she thought about Conner and smiled to herself when she realized that Conner was a sexy mixture of mountain man and nerd.

They'd had several conversations that had proven to her that he could hold his own in business. He knew a lot about his family's businesses, and she knew he'd filled in at both the restaurant and Jordan Shipping.

She believed that it was one of the reasons he'd been undecided as to what field he wanted to go into. He'd been mentally pulled in so many directions and had so many choices that he couldn't make up his mind. Choosing the Coast Guard had been the easiest route to take. Or at least that's how it seemed after hearing him talk about it.

After calling down to the Golden Oar and placing their dinner orders, she shot a text off to Conner to let him know that their dinner would be ready soon. He sent a text back almost immediately that he would grab it and be there soon, then he asked how she was feeling.

"Better. Rested," she replied.

"Good. Sore?" he texted back.

She assessed herself once more and answered.

"No, I think I worked out all the kinks."

"Good. See you soon," he sent back.

She busied herself by setting the table and making sure everything was in place.

"Wow." Robin came out from her bedroom and glanced around. "This place is coming along." She walked over and hugged her.

"Yes, it is." She looked around and was happily surprised at how wonderful the small space looked and felt. It was starting to feel more like home. She no longer cared if she went barefoot in the main part of the house, since she'd rolled out several large area rugs that she'd found in the Jordan barn. She had yet to pull up the carpet in her bedroom but had laid a few rugs around so she could feel more comfortable.

By the time Conner arrived with the food, she was starving and tired once more.

"Do I smell chocolate cookies?" Conner asked, walking into the dining room with the bag of containers holding their dinner.

"Yes." She smiled as she sat down, realizing that her leg was aching again, probably from all the cleaning and baking she'd done.

He turned and frowned down at her. "You're overexerting yourself." He reached up and laid a hand on her shoulder. She could see the worry in his eyes.

"I'm fine." She motioned to the food. "But starving."

He smiled and then nodded towards Robin as he pulled out the containers of food.

Dinner was nice. It was warming to see that Conner could easily get along with and even joke with her sister. They talked about the land and the possibility of their folks moving there. Then he mentioned that he'd visited his uncle and aunt, who were apparently old friends of their parents.

"We've known Megan and Todd for as long as we can remember," Robin replied. "They're like our long-lost relatives," she joked. "At one point, I used to call them aunt and uncle. Then my mother corrected me when I was a teenager." Her sister laughed suddenly. "I had to do a family tree for school and didn't know exactly where they fit into our family. The next time we came to Pride, I was embarrassed." Robin sighed. "And disappointed at the same time."

"Until I was eight, I believed I had three moms and dads," Conner joked back. "My cousins were all my brothers and sisters. I was upset when my cousin Suzie was born, and I couldn't take her home to live with us." He chuckled.

"We have a few cousins we'd like to ignore," Robin said, glancing at her, making her chuckle.

"Carl and Steven." She rolled her eyes. "Our mother's brother's kids. Not that they're terrors, it's just... they are boys," she added, feeling a little stupid.

"Growing up, they were our arch nemeses," Robin added. "They would mess up our dolls, take over every game we played, and usually push one or both of us into mud puddles each visit."

"Carl is going to law school and Steve is a DJ for a local radio station," Kara informed him. "And both of them would still find any reason to push us into the mud if given the chance."

Robin laughed and poured herself another glass of wine.

Kara had already had two glasses, which had helped her leg muscles relax again. She was thankful that she was feeling comfortably numb at this point. After finishing off the rest of the lasagna that she'd ordered, she leaned back and tried not to slide out of the chair.

"You look tired," Robin told her after a moment.

Kara realized she'd grown quiet and had been listening to Robin and Conner chatting.

"I am," she realized. "It was a long day."

"How's the leg?" Conner asked.

She wiggled her calf and winced slightly. "Sore, but I've had worse. I used to play soccer in grade school and had shin splints a few times."

"Ouch." Conner winced. "Not fun." He stood up and started clearing the table.

"Let me do that." Robin jumped up. "You picked up the

food, Kara baked the cookies and cleaned up beforehand, the least I can do is dishes." Robin took all of the plates and disappeared into the kitchen.

"Bring back the plate of cookies," she called out. She turned to Conner. "I could use the sugar."

"How about we go into the living room and relax. You can put your leg up," he suggested.

She started to get up and he was there, helping her out of the chair, guiding her to the sofa. He nudged her down and sat beside her. Then he pulled her leg up into his lap and slid up her legging to see the massive bruise that covered her skin.

She winced at the purple and red skin.

"Ouch," Robin said, coming into the room, holding a plate of cookies. "That looks worse than you let on."

"Do you have an ice pack?" Conner asked Robin.

Kara groaned. "I think I froze my leg earlier," she said to him when he glanced in her direction.

"It'll help with the pain," he suggested as Robin disappeared back into the kitchen.

"Bring me a glass of milk," she called out as she reached for a cookie.

"Make that two," Conner called after her, making her smile. "What?" he asked her when he noticed.

"I like that you get along with my sister," she said softly.

"I get along great with most sisters," he admitted as he started to rub the spots around the bruise on her leg. Then his hands stilled. "Why? Did you date someone who didn't get along with Robin?"

Robin had walked in at that moment and laughed, getting Conner's attention.

"That fits the description of every guy Kara's dated." She handed Conner a glass of milk and then gave Kara one before taking the bag of frozen peas from under her arm and setting it gently down on Kara's bruised calf.

Since Kara was twisted on the sofa, the makeshift ice pack only covered half of her sore muscle. Still, she figured it was better than nothing since she couldn't manage to enjoy her cookie and milk without spilling.

"Oh?" Conner asked, leaning back to enjoy the treat and conversation. "I'm all ears."

Kara groaned as her sister started telling her current boyfriend about her past mistakes. Conner chuckled at some of her sister's stories and, after finishing off two cookies and setting down her half empty milk, Kara twisted slightly as Conner started rubbing her leg again.

She hadn't realized she'd fallen asleep until Conner picked her up some time later.

"Hm?" she moaned and tried to focus her eyes.

"Shh, I'm just carrying you to bed," he said softly.

"Okay." She smiled and wrapped her arms around his neck. "You're going to stay?"

"Not tonight," he answered with a sigh as he maneuvered her through her bedroom doorway. "I have work early in the morning and then I'm going to finish moving into my new apartment."

"M-kay," she said as he laid her down on the bed.

He sat beside her on the bed and leaned down to place a soft kiss on her lips. "Thank you for dinner."

"You're the one who got the food," she reminded him as she looked up at him. The darkness of the room cast shadows over his features, making him look even more handsome and a little mysterious.

"Then thanks for hosting and for the cookies, " he replied with a chuckle. "They were delicious. The best cookies I've had."

She snort-laughed and then gasped as she covered her mouth with her hand. "Sorry."

His smile grew. "Don't be, that was the sexiest thing I've heard all day."

"You can go now," she said as she felt her face heat. She was thankful for the darkness of the room.

She heard him chuckle again, and then he leaned in and placed a soft kiss on her lips. "Goodnight."

She warmed from the kiss and relaxed again. "Night," she said with a sigh and fell back asleep.

CHAPTER SIXTEEN

By the time Conner started unloading his things from the back of his truck, big snowflakes fell from the gray sky and covered the ground and everything else. His brother and his cousin George were helping him move some of his bigger items later that weekend. For now, he'd sleep on his air mattress on the floor and make do with what he could carry himself.

He was happily surprised to see Kara walk up to him in the grocery store parking lot shortly after he'd finished taking up the last load of his stuff.

"Hey." He walked over and wrapped his arms around her and then kissed her. "What are you doing here?"

"I came to see if I could help," she said, frowning over at his empty truck bed. "Is that everything?"

He chuckled. "No, this is just the end of the first load. I'll have some muscle help later this weekend to move the bigger items."

"Oh." She frowned slightly.

"Did you walk here?"

"It's only about a block away. What can I help with?"

He thought about it. How she'd been bruised and tired last night and shook his head. "You can cheer me on," he said, but the look she gave him let him know instantly that she wouldn't sit on the sidelines easily. "How about you head into the store and grab me a coffee?" he asked, realizing that this might be the last load he could cart from the house today if the snow continued to fall at this pace.

"Okay," she said, rubbing her hands together. Then she leaned up and kissed him again and smiled up at him.

He felt his entire body heat, which had him emptying the rest of the truck in record time. When he'd set the last item on the kitchen counter of his new place, Kara walked in with a tray of drinks and a box from the bakery down the street.

"Why get regular coffee when you can have an extra sugary drink with pastries?" she joked as she set the box down on his counter next to the lamp that he'd set there moments before.

"Here." He pulled over a couple of the barstools he'd grabbed from the barn so they could sit next to each other. "At least I was smart enough to grab these." He took a sip of the coffee and looked down at it. "My favorite. How'd you know?"

She chuckled. "I cheated and asked Becca. She and Sara know everyone in town's favorite drinks and pastries." She opened the box.

He smiled down at the bear claws inside. "I swear if either of those sisters was around my age and single, I'd marry them."

Kara laughed. "Both of them?"

He shrugged. "Then again, Becca's daughter Brook is single."

Kara narrowed her eyes and poked him in the chest with her finger, causing him to laugh.

"And like a little sister to me," he finished as he wrapped his arm around her.

"She is awfully cute," Kara supplied.

"She's too chipper in the morning. I think it comes from working at the bakery all her life. Days where I work early and head over there for a pick-me-up, she's always smiling and talking."

Kara laughed. "Not a morning person?"

"At four in the morning?"

"Four?" Kara gasped. "What are you doing up at four?"

He thought about all his early mornings and shrugged. "Training the new recruits."

"As in... teaching them?"

"Yeah. Allen Masters took me under his wing last year and, well, now he's bumped me up to second in charge of training. He claims I have a knack for teaching. Don't get too excited. I just make the newbs run around, do drills, and stuff like that." He took another bite of the bear claw and relaxed back to watch the snow fall outside the massive windows that overlooked the main street of Pride.

Kara glanced over his shoulder at the empty space. "Wow, this place is bigger than I thought it would be."

"I'll give you a tour." He stood up and finished off his sugary treat quickly. "It only has one bedroom, but the space is pretty big."

He showed her the bedroom and newly remodeled bathroom.

"Wow," she gasped as she looked at the massive walk-in shower. "I can only dream of having a shower this nice."

"Yeah, Parker's revamp." He enjoyed the tall glass walls

surrounding the new shower. "It's got three shower heads." He reached in and turned on the water.

"Nice. This entire bathroom is what dreams are made of." She turned around slightly then ran a finger over the new marble countertops and sinks.

"Anytime you want to have a sleepover," he said, wrapping his arms around her waist and pulling her in for another kiss. The way she melted against his chest had him wishing he had more than just a mattress on the floor of his new bedroom. Hell, he didn't even have sheets on it yet. This thought kept him from taking the kiss deeper. Instead, he pulled back and motioned towards the closet. "It's got plenty of closet space too."

She narrowed her eyes. "Just how long do you want me to sleep over for?"

He shrugged. "As long as you want." He ran a hand up her arm. "I don't feel like I'm going to tire of this for a while. You?"

She shook her head as she looked up at him. "No, me either."

She turned away from him but before she did so, he noticed her cheeks turning a soft shade of pink.

"Wow," she gasped as she stepped into the walk-in closet. "This could be another bedroom."

He chuckled. "Yeah, I doubt I'm going to fill a quarter of it with my stuff."

"I don't think I could even fill half of it," she admitted.

After that, they went back into the living room and looked out at the snow falling over Main Street.

"On a clear day, you can see Pride harbor." He motioned into the gray mist that surrounded the small town.

"I bet. Even this view is beautiful." She wrapped her

arms around herself as she looked out. "It's getting worse out there."

"Yeah, we're supposed to have about a foot before morning."

She was silent for a while. "We have another wedding this weekend. We're expecting snow the entire time." She sighed. "They've rented a horse and sleigh to drive them through town. It should be perfectly romantic."

"Winter weddings are nice," he said with a shrug. "Course nothing beats a grassy yard, like the one we stood in yesterday, overlooking the beach in the spring."

Her eyebrows shot up and she turned to him. "Oh?"

He shrugged. "Sure. I mean, you add a bunch of flowers, like Suzie had."

Kara chuckled. "She does own a flower shop," she reminded him.

"Yeah, but you put them in a freshly cut grassy yard looking down at the water, the dramatic view as a backdrop..."

She tilted her head. "You're an artist like your mother."

He chuckled. "I've been accused of that a lot."

"It's true." She turned towards him and ran her eyes over him. "Tell me more." She motioned for him to go on.

"Well." He thought about it, about the day he'd dreamed of marrying the woman of his dreams. "Okay, so it would be a whole day affair. Early morning breakfast on the lawn. Time to enjoy visiting with family and friends, followed by games and fun events for any young kids. Everyone always forgets the kids." He shook his head, remembering how his niece and nephew had to stay at a babysitter for the last two events. "Then, enough time for everyone to head back and change for an early evening wedding as the sun sets behind the ceremony, followed by a candlelit dinner and party after."

"Sounds perfect," she said with a sigh.

He hadn't realized he'd pulled her close and wrapped his arms around her while he'd described his ideal wedding.

In his fantasy, he'd imagined Kara as the perfect bride. Which startled him and caused him to drop his arms from around her waist.

"I'll... drive you home," he heard himself saying suddenly.

How could he get so lost in thought that he'd started daydreaming about marrying Kara? Not that he didn't have feelings for her, but thinking about marrying her this soon? That was just crazy. Right?

After dropping her off at the cottage, he headed back to his folks' place to grab a few more clothes and essentials so that he could spend his first night at his own place.

He was surprised to see his parents up watching an old movie. He was pretty sure they'd been necking on the sofa and had pulled away when his mother had heard him enter the house. When he came back downstairs with a backpack full of his last personal effects thrown over his shoulder, his mother was standing in the kitchen with a large, framed painting wrapped in shipping paper. He'd seen enough of her artwork ready to be shipped out to understand it was one of her pieces.

"A home warming gift," she said in response to his questioning look.

Pulling off the wrapping paper, he smiled down at one of his favorite paintings of his mother's. The lighthouse, which sat less than fifteen minutes outside of Pride, had always been one of his favorite views of the Oregon coast. There were two small figures walking towards the lighthouse, which he'd always assumed were his parents before they had kids.

From what would be his new backyard soon, you could just make out the lighthouse in the distance. It was one of the reasons he'd picked the lot for himself.

"Thank you." He set the painting down and walked over to wrap his arms around his mother.

"I've made you some meals," his father signed from across the room. "They're in the freezer."

Conner chuckled and signed back. "I'm not moving across the state. I'm only going three miles away. Not to mention I'll be living above a grocery store."

"Yeah," his dad signed back, "but you know how your mother is." His father smiled sweetly as his mother narrowed her eyes at him.

"I've put them in a paper bag in the freezer." His mother turned her attention back to him and said. "You can grab it on your way out."

He stopped short of rolling his eyes at his parents coddling. But since he wanted the free home-cooked meals, he placed a kiss on his mother's cheek, grabbed his new painting, and headed out.

"Don't forget dinner at your sister's this weekend," his mother called after him.

"Right," he called back.

Both Riley and Lilly had texted everyone in the family last week with a formal invitation to dinner over at Riley and Carter's place. Carter had purchased a classic Victorian home that sat on one of the small cliffs that overlooked the town shortly after moving to Pride. The home was big enough to easily host every single one of the Jordan clan.

"Oh, and Conner?" His mother stopped him as he was

halfway out the garage door, his hand still on the door handle.

"Yeah?"

"Bring Kara," she called out.

"Right," he said and shut the door in case his mother had any more instructions.

Driving back to his own place, he couldn't help but smile. If his family was expecting him to bring Kara, that meant that they already liked her.

How many girls had he tried to inaugurate into his family over the years? The Jordans got along great with anyone and everyone, except when it was a girl that he'd brought home as a date. Then they'd turned into a pack of hyenas, which, he knew, was ironically called a clan, like his family.

Not that they were rude to his dates. Hell, most of the girls he'd dated in high school still lived in Pride and dealt with his family on a regular basis. Some of them were even still friends with his cousins.

As he settled down later on his queen-sized air mattress in the middle of his new bedroom floor, he thought about how Kara already fit in with his family members. After all, she'd organized two of their weddings, not to mention several of the family's other events as well.

His mind must have been on Kara as he fell asleep since his dreams were filled with her and images of the perfect wedding he'd described to her earlier. But when a dark shadow fell over the crowd at the event and lightning struck, he jolted in his sleep as his mind tried to warn him that something was coming.

CHAPTER SEVENTEEN

The next few days, Kara busied herself with her normal daily routines. Prep work for the upcoming events was slightly hindered by the fresh foot of snow. She'd have to drive the old truck to and from the flower shop the evening before their next event.

The new heater was working overtime in the massive barn, as was the large gas fireplace, in order to heat up the space for the middle school dance they were hosting Friday night.

As she walked around, watching the awkward kids asking one another to dance or avoiding asking each other, she thought about Conner.

Each night after he'd gotten off work, he'd either stopped by to see her or he'd called and talked to her for as long as he could. He'd helped them pull up the carpet in the rest of the house and had replaced the rest of the cabinet doors in the kitchen. Now every room in the cottage looked and felt like home.

He'd even invited her to a family dinner on Sunday

night up at his sister and Carter's place. Which had to mean something. Didn't it?

She'd been over to Riley and Carter's beautiful home several times already, but this would be her first official Jordan clan dinner invite. She needed to make a good impression. Not that she hadn't already been around his family plenty of times before, but this was just... different. This would be the first event since she'd officially started dating Conner.

She remembered how nice Allison had been to her that day on the beach and how she'd gone out of her way to let her pick out the furniture she wanted from the barn.

Then again, everyone in Pride knew how wonderful and generous Allison Jordan was. Rumors were that she'd given more than a million dollars of her art income last year to a charity that helped deaf children. Of course, with the subject being so close to her heart, everyone automatically assumed the rumors were true.

Everyone knew that Allison's paintings easily sold for those high figures. Kara could imagine the woman giving even more than that to help out someone in need. She was just that generous of a person.

She'd only met Conner's father a few times. She hadn't spoken to him directly since she didn't know sign language very well. Outside of the basic ABCs she'd learned in summer camp one year, she also knew a few other words like mother, father, and sister.

Still, she'd heard enough about the man to know that he was just as kind as the rest of the family. It was obvious that Conner got his looks from his father. He was tall like Iian Jordan and had similar features. Still, Kara could see a lot of Allison in him as well. Conner's dark curly hair had come from his mother, as well as his blue eyes.

She was thankful that her sister had taken the hint every time Conner had showed up and had disappeared with her laptop to work.

Kara had met Conner at Baked, the local pizza shop, one evening for dinner. Corey and Carter Miller, twin brothers who had married cousins Riley and Lilly, owned the pizzeria.

Most everyone in town could tell the identical brothers apart at this point. Kara could usually guess who was who as long as they didn't switch jobs on her. Corey worked the counter while Carter was usually hanging out in the back, overseeing the kitchen.

She knew that Conner's brother and sister, Riley and Jacob, were fraternal twins, but the pair were as different as day and night. Riley was shorter and had flyaway bleached blonde hair with a bubbly personality while Jacob... Well, the best way Kara could describe him was dark, brooding, and outdoorsy.

Speaking of brooding, Kara was in a funk herself. Since last weekend, she'd been hoping for another night with Conner. Whenever they were around one another, she just couldn't keep that night out of her mind.

She understood that he had very early mornings on the days that he worked and couldn't stay up late. She was very thankful for the time she did get with him during the week and was looking forward to seeing more of him that weekend. She was even planning on trying to convince him to let her stay at his place after the family dinner.

She knew that he was moving the rest of his things into the apartment that night after he got off work. She'd thought about sneaking out of the dance to go help him move, but then she'd caught several of the boys trying to spike the juice with a small bottle of rum and knew that she was needed at the dance instead.

She couldn't imagine getting sued because all of the kids in attendance had ended up drunk.

Looking back at her own childhood, she couldn't imagine doing something like that. Both she and Robin had been quiet and amenable children. There had never been a time when either of them had caused or gotten in any trouble. Maybe it was their cousins' influence that caused the sisters to want to be better?

"Were we this awkward?" Robin whispered as she stopped next to her.

Kara glanced over at her sister and chuckled. "Maybe you were." She shrugged. "I was never awkward."

Robin laughed. "Right, and I suppose I'm the one who broke my wrist trying to play football to impress a boy?"

Kara rolled her eyes. "I was eleven and in love."

Robin smiled. "And Sean Wilson didn't even notice you."

"Jerk," she added without conviction.

"He owns several animal rescue sites now," Robin reminded her.

"Right, he's a jerk that's kind to animals."

"I would have thought that you'd be over helping Conner move tonight," Robin said.

"I'm needed here."

Robin glanced around and motioned to several of the parent chaperones. "I think we've got it covered. Actually, I think I have tomorrow night and Sunday morning's events covered as well." She bumped hips with her and winked. "If you get my drift. You've been in a funk, and I think Conner has the cure."

Kara's heart did a little flip at the idea of heading over to be with Conner again. Of being able to spend the next few days with him.

Her sister nudged her shoulder again. "Go on. Go be with your boy toy."

"Are you sure?" Kara asked.

"Yeah, someone around here has got to get some and since I have no prospects in sight, it might as well be you. Take the truck though. It's still snowing out there." She motioned to the large barn doors that were currently shutting out the cold. "If I need it tomorrow, I'll stop by and get it with my spare keys."

"Thanks." She knew better than to argue with her sister when she was being tossed a bone.

Rushing from the back door of the barn and heading down the newly lit pathway towards the cottage, she realized she'd forgotten her coat earlier when a large clump of snow landed on her head, causing a shiver to race down her spine.

She let herself in the back door of the cottage and raced around and gathered up what she expected she'd need to stay over.

She debated over the sexy new pink nighty she'd purchased with Conner in mind and figured she would save that for a special occasion. This was, after all, a spur of the moment decision. She hadn't even messaged him to tell him she was coming over.

The one other time she'd done that with a boyfriend, he'd had another woman over that night. Being cheated on sucked. Especially when you were pretty sure the guy was the one. She'd spent most of her senior year in high school planning out her very own perfect wedding. But Ben had cheated on her and secretly joined the military. He'd left her the day after she'd found out his secret.

Maybe that's why she had decided to get out of Portland.

But Conner was not like Ben. Not in the least.

SHE THREW a few other things into her overnight bag, grabbed the truck keys, and headed out, only to come up short when the truck wouldn't start. She tried everything she knew to get the old thing to turn over. Kicking the tire for good measure, she grabbed her overnight bag. The snow and broken truck weren't going to stop her from having the Friday night she wanted.

She sent her sister a text message updating her on the truck situation and headed out towards Conner's place.

It wasn't as if Pride was unsafe. Actually, a few years back it had been voted the safest small town in all of Oregon, an award the town had been very proud of.

It wasn't the people or crime Kara was worried about as she hit the halfway mark, it was the cold. She'd grabbed her thick winter coat and had slipped on her snow boots and gloves before heading out, but when a gust of wind blew right through her, she wished she'd had the foresight to grab a scarf as well.

She was so preoccupied with keeping the wind at bay that, at first, she didn't notice the truck following behind her. It wasn't until she'd passed the closed flower shop, All in Bloom, that she noticed the truck reflected in the darkened store's glass.

She normally wouldn't have worried, but the dark blue color reminded her instantly of the truck that had almost hit her and Conner up at the property.

She stopped at the flower shop and faked as if she was looking at the pretty display inside while actually watching the truck's reflection in the glass. When it stopped just behind her, she pulled out her cell phone and, in a very loud voice, pretended to answer a call.

"Hey, no, I'm just outside the flower shop," she said to herself as she watched the passenger side door open slightly. It hung there while she acted as if she was listening to someone. "Yeah, I'll be there in two minutes. Is everyone else already there?" she asked loudly. "Okay, I'm just outside the floral shop. I'll see you soon." She put her phone back in her pocket and took off at a quick pace towards Conner's place.

She didn't look back to see what the truck did or if anyone had even gotten out. Instead, she half sprinted down the rest of the block until she could see the bright grocery store sign just ahead of her through the thick falling snow.

She saw Conner's truck in the parking lot and relaxed slightly. She was heading towards the stairs when a hand gripped her arm, and she screamed at the top of her lungs.

"Wow." Conner jumped away from Kara quickly. A flood of concern washed over him when he noticed how pale she looked and how scared she obviously was. "What's going on?" he asked, taking her in his arms and scanning the snow-covered parking lot.

"The truck... I think it was following me," she said into his shoulder. He felt her shivering and started to pull her up the stairs to his apartment. He'd run downstairs to get some basic groceries and had spotted her rushing across the street through the windows. He'd left all his groceries in the cart to greet her.

At first, he'd been prepared to scold her about walking in the middle of a snowstorm, but after she'd screamed, he was too concerned to lecture her.

She stood there as he shut them inside the apartment.

"I'm going to warm you up while I wait for Aiden to get here." He pulled out his cell phone and shot a text message to Aiden, letting him know what had happened.

Kara stood in place with her arms wrapped around her

and continued to shiver. Her soft pink hat hadn't saved most of her hair from the snow and long strands of her hair were soaked and falling over her shoulders. Her jacket and pants were now as wet as the rest of her since the warmth of his apartment had melted the snowflakes that had covered her.

"Here." He helped her remove her wet jacket and hat, then hung them on the hooks by the door. "Come over and sit down on the sofa. I'll make you something warm to drink." He nudged her towards the sofa and then covered her with a throw blanket. Leaning down, he removed her boots and set them by the front door as well.

Just as he put a pot of water on the stove, there was a knock on his door, and Kara jumped and gasped.

"Easy, it's just Aiden," he assured her.

"Evening." His cousin Suzie's husband, the chief of police for Pride, stepped into his apartment. Aiden was also a longtime friend.

Not too long ago, Aiden had lived in this very apartment. Now, he and Suzie were living in a rental house until their new home was finished being built up near the property where his own home would be soon.

"Hey." He motioned to where Kara was sitting on the sofa, looking wide-eyed and cold.

"I drove past the flower shop. Everything looked locked up. No sign of the blue truck anywhere in town," Aiden said quickly.

"It was the same truck," Kara chimed in. "I know it was."

"I don't doubt it. I just wanted to stop off and see if you happened to grab the make or model or by chance the plate number?" Aiden asked.

Kara quickly shook her head. "No, sorry. I was..." She

swallowed and glanced at Conner. "I couldn't think. I pretended to be on a phone call when the man started to get out of the passenger side."

Conner tensed. "Someone was coming at you?" he asked, feeling his blood begin to boil.

"N-no. I..." She shook her head. "I pretended to look in the flower shop windows and saw them pull up behind me. Then the passenger door opened and... I took off running." She looked down at her hands.

Conner walked over and sat next to her, taking her cold hands into his own. "That was a smart move," he assured her before turning back to Aiden. "She's frozen. I'm going to see about warming her up."

Aiden nodded. "I've got everyone on shift driving around town looking out for the truck. I'll keep you posted." He nodded to Kara. "It might be best, at least for a while, if you didn't walk alone after dark."

"Thanks," she said quickly before Aiden left.

"How about some soup? My dad made a few meals for me and his homemade chicken soup is one of them. I can head down and grab a loaf of bread? I was getting a few other things when I spotted you."

Kara nodded as she continued to look down at her hands.

"Hey," he started, only to stop when the tea kettle started whistling. Standing up, he poured her a cup of hot chocolate and then returned to her side. She held onto the mug as if using it to warm her entire body.

His eyes zoned in on the overnight bag that she'd set down just inside his doorway and he smiled.

"You could have called me. I would've come over and picked you up," he suggested.

Her eyes flashed to his. "I was going to drive, but... the truck wouldn't start."

He reached up and brushed his hand down her cold cheeks. "Why don't you drink your hot chocolate, then head in and enjoy a hot shower? I'll heat us up some soup and bread and then we can snuggle on the sofa and watch a movie."

Her eyes met his and she sighed with relief and relaxed slightly. "That sounds... amazing," she said with a smile.

He leaned in and brushed his lips across hers. "I'll be right back," he promised her.

He made sure to lock his door behind him as he went back downstairs to the grocery store.

Patty O'Neil was a staple in Pride. Anyone who stepped foot in the small town knew who the woman was. Even more, Patty knew everything there was to know about everyone in her town.

"What spooked Kara?" Patty asked him when he returned to get his almost-full cart of food.

"Someone followed her over here," he answered with a shrug, causing Patty to frown.

"Think it was the same someone who hit her with rocks the other week?" Patty asked.

He didn't even bother asking how she'd heard of the incident at the property. He shrugged and replied, "Sounds like it." He turned towards the bread aisle. "Got any French bread left?"

"Sure," Patty called after him. "On the last shelf on the left."

At this time of night, he and Patty were the only two people in the store. He'd caught her moments before she was going to lock up and head home.

He grabbed a loaf of the freshly made bread and added a few more items to the cart, then paid and headed back upstairs with his arms full.

Hearing the shower running, he took his time putting everything away in his cupboards and then heated up the container of soup his dad had packed for him. At this point, he'd pretty much gone through everything his folks had made for him. Which is why he'd been down at the store getting more supplies when he'd spotted Kara running through the snow.

He'd only had the soup left and had planned on eating it alone that night after everyone had finished helping him move everything into the apartment.

He'd spent almost an hour putting things in place but still, there were boxes of his things piled along the living room and bedroom walls. He'd finished bringing over his clothes and he'd been correct in his assessment—his items didn't even take up a quarter of the massive closet.

He heard the shower turn off and smiled at the thought of Kara, naked in his shower. Of being able to fall asleep with her wrapped around him like before.

He almost burned the bread he was heating up in the oven, daydreaming about the coming night with Kara. Thankfully, he remembered it just in time and was pulling it from the oven when she stepped out of the bedroom dressed in tight black leggings and an oversized sweater that hung off her left shoulder.

She'd tied her long-wet hair in an intricate braid that lay over her other shoulder. She'd freshened up her face and no longer looked pale and scared.

He smiled at her. "Feel better?" he asked as she moved over to sit at the bar top.

"Yes, thank you." She nodded to the bread. "That smells amazing."

"The soup or the bread?" he joked as he set a bowl in front of her. He set the bread on a wood chopping block and grabbed a knife from the drawer. "How about some wine?" He pulled a bottle of red wine from his fridge. "I just bought this downstairs and it's not that cold yet, but..." He shrugged.

"It will be perfect," she assured him as he opened the bottle and poured them each a glass before sitting down next to her with his own bowl of soup. "Man, your dad can cook," she said after taking the first bite of soup.

He broke off a piece of bread and then dipped it in the soup. "Yeah, it's a miracle me and my sister and brother didn't weigh a ton growing up. Then again, when I was eight, I was significantly chubby."

She chuckled. "I can't see that."

"Oh, it's true. I have the pictures to prove it," he said between bites.

"I was too skinny and too tall," she replied with a frown. "Boys used to make fun of me all the time. Well, at least until they finally outgrew me in junior high."

"Most girls grow up faster than boys. I remember when Riley used to be as tall as I was."

She almost choked on a bite. "What is Riley? All of five-two?"

He chuckled. "Five-four and I hit six foot at eighteen."

She narrowed her eyes. "You're what? Six-five now?"

"Six-four. I grew another inch just last year. My uncle Aaron claims that most men don't stop growing until their mid-twenties." He shrugged. "Boys are stupid if they make fun of girls because they grow faster than us."

"Oh, like you never made fun of your sister or cousins?" She nudged him on the leg, causing him to smile.

"Oh, I made fun of them plenty of times, but never about their height. I guess I always figured I'd eventually be taller than them. After all, it runs in the family."

She chuckled and shook her head. "It must have been wonderful growing up with so many kids in the family."

"At times, yes." He was more interested in watching her than remembering all the good times growing up. "What about you?"

"As I've mentioned, our cousins didn't live too far from us, but they were... well, boys." She rolled her eyes and held in a chuckle.

He smiled. "You know, that's one thing the Jordan clan never had issues with. The whole boys versus girls issue. I suppose it was my aunt Lacey's doing. She insisted on showing us that anything a boy could do, she and any of the girls could do as well."

"Even become Mayor?" Kara added.

"Especially that," he added with a laugh. "Do you know, she's been the best thing for Pride. The budget has been balanced every year she's been in office, and the growth of the town has been on a steady incline. We aren't losing businesses like some other small towns."

"Speaking of that." Kara pushed her empty bowl away. "I meant to tell you that I can officially say it was Thomas Carson who bumped into me a few weeks ago and posed as a lawyer."

He tensed. "It was? How do you know?"

"I pulled up a picture from the C&C Investment website."

"Okay, so, what? Pose as a lawyer to..." He shook his head trying to run over the reasons. "I don't get it."

"Neither did we. Robin thinks he's wanting to do a time-share scam in Pride. You know, build a bunch of condos and a resort and then sell them off to multiple people who only get to visit one week out of the year. Half the time the place sits empty because people don't travel or decide to go somewhere else."

"Time shares aren't really scams. I mean, legally they're allowed," he pointed out.

"Yeah, I get that, but in Pride?" She shook her head. "I just can't see it."

"Okay, let's set that aside for a moment. The real question that we should be asking is why he was snooping around your land, posing as a lawyer? Has he come back since then?"

"No." She shook her head and tucked one of her legs underneath her as she sipped her wine. "You don't think that was him in the truck, do you?"

He thought about it, about what Aiden had told him about the man and shook his head. "From what I've heard, Carson doesn't like to get his hands dirty. Most likely, he's hired someone. Which is why I'm surprised he was the one to stop by and talk to you himself. It just doesn't add up. The last my uncle heard from the guy, he was sniffing around some land out by the state park." He thought about it, then decided that he didn't want the rest of his time with Kara to be spoiled. "What do you say we take the wine and brownies I bought over to the sofa and watch a movie, then neck a little," he said with a grin.

She chuckled. "I like that idea." Just as they got up to move over to the sofa, her cell phone rang.

"It's Robin," she said with a frown. "I... didn't call her when I got here." She answered it and stepped into the bedroom for some privacy. From what he could gather, her sister was upset at what had happened.

Since he had time, he called Aiden to get an update.

"Any updates?" he asked when Aiden answered.

"No," Aiden answered with a sigh. "We've been all over Pride and short of a few tire marks in the snow, haven't spotted anything. They could be on the other side of Edgeview by now. But we'll keep looking."

"Good. Hey..." He glanced towards the bedroom door. "Just another update. Kara told me that Carson paid her a visit two weeks ago. He posed as a lawyer with a client interested in purchasing their land."

"Seriously?" Aiden said. "When was this?"

Conner thought about it and gave him the date. "Kara said it was during one of the events at the barn and that she'd run into him on the pathway between the cottage and the venue." He walked over to look out over the snow-covered town and saw a patrol car drive slowly by. Everyone in town had pretty much called it a night at this point. Even Patty had left to go home, leaving the store beneath his feet dark. Only the streetlights and the patrol car showed life outside his window. The snow was too thick to see a few feet past the last streetlamp or beyond the buildings.

"Guess we need to find out why he's interested in their place now too. I'll talk to Todd in the morning," Aiden added.

"How's construction on your place going?" Conner asked, changing the subject.

"Slow, now that the weather has come in. But they're getting most of it done. Might be in it by Christmas. I heard you'll be building up in Hidden Cove?"

He chuckled. "Yeah, I might be in by next Christmas."

"Well, until then, the apartment is a great place. I have fond memories of living there," Aiden added.

"Yeah, I'm enjoying it so far." He heard Kara get off the phone with her sister. "I'll let you go. Thanks for checking things out tonight."

"No problem. Oh, and you may want to make sure Kara stays off the streets at night."

"Will do," he added before hanging up.

"Did he just say I needed to stay off the streets at night, like I'm some sort of...?" Kara surprised him by being directly behind him.

He jumped a little and winced slightly. "Yeah, um, he didn't mean..."

"He makes it sound like I was..." She shook her head and crossed her arms over her chest.

"Listen." He touched her shoulders and pulled her closer. "Aiden didn't mean it like that. Trust me. He's not the smoothest guy I know. I have no idea what Suzie sees in him," he said with a smile.

Kara's eyes narrowed. "Then you must be blind. Outside of his rude comments, he's one of the sexiest men in Pride."

Conner's eyebrows shot up as his eyes narrowed. "Oh?"

Kara smiled slightly. "Sure. I mean, if a woman likes the tall, dark, broody, sex-in-a-uniform type." She shrugged slightly and tilted her head, as if she were thinking about something. "I mean, if he wasn't a married man..."

"You'd what?" he asked, feeling his defenses go up.

She chuckled. "I'd probably bash his head in after the statement he just made. He made it seem like I was a..." She dropped off again and he waited.

"A what?" he teased.

She narrowed her eyes at him again. "You know what," she almost hissed.

He laughed and pulled her into a hug.

"So, now that we know what type of man you like... Do I happen to fit into that category?"

"Well, I don't know. I have yet to see you in a uniform."

"That could be arranged." He leaned down and kissed her.

CHAPTER NINETEEN

Okay, so any man who could knock her socks off just kissing her was definingly her type. It had taken her almost half an hour under the very hot spray in his shower to warm herself up earlier. What she should have done was have him kiss her like he was doing now.

Every fiber of her body was sizzling when he finally pulled back and looked down at her.

"So, I know I suggested a movie and brownies..." he said as he ran his eyes over her face. "But what I want to do is take you into the bedroom instead."

"Great minds think alike," she said quickly. "I want that too." She smiled as she took his hand and started walking back to his bedroom.

"Everything okay with your sister?" he asked before they got too far.

"Yes," she answered with a sigh. "Conner?" She turned towards him after stepping into his bedroom.

"Hm?" he asked, his hands going to her hips as his body bumped up against hers.

"Let's not talk about my sister right now." She reached

up on her toes to kiss him again. The way his hands were running over her hips had her melting in his arms. Her fingernails dug into his muscular shoulders, pulling him towards the bed in the middle of the room.

She noticed that he finally had a bed frame put together but had yet to move it up against a wall.

When the back of her legs bumped up against the mattress, she laughed as she started falling backwards.

Their bodies landed in a heap as he continued to hold onto her.

"That was smooth." He groaned. "Sorry about that. I forgot I hadn't moved the bed to the wall yet."

She held on and smiled up at him. "It's okay. I was getting too heated anyway." She ran a finger over his stubble-covered chin.

"I would have shaved if I'd known you were coming over." He ran his fingertip over her chin. "I'm scratching you." He moved to get up.

"No." She held him in place, enjoying his weight pinning her down. "I like it." She ran her hand over his face now. "It's sexy. Besides, it makes you look forbidden and manly." She wiggled her eyebrows, causing him to chuckle.

Then she was pulling him back down and kissing him.

"I've wanted you here, in my bed," he said against her neck as he ran his mouth over her skin.

He nudged her sweater further down her shoulder and trailed kisses over her exposed skin as his hands moved up under the sweater, cupping her.

A moan of delight escaped her lips as he played with her nipples, causing them to stand erect for him.

"Conner," she sighed as she wrapped her legs around his hips. She pulled him closer to her as she pulled his shirt over his head so she could enjoy running her hands over his toned muscles and tan skin. She didn't know how he was still so tan at this point but enjoyed licking her way up his shoulder to start nibbling on his ear as his hands moved lower and tugged the leggings down her hips.

Then he cupped her, and she arched into his hand. His name was a sigh from her lips as he slid a finger into her slick pussy. She'd wanted him, wanted this, since the last time they'd been together. She'd dreamed about being with him every night since then.

"Hang onto me," he groaned as he shifted slightly so that he could suck her nipple into his mouth. His fingers moved with the same rhythm of his mouth on her breast. "Let go," he begged as she felt herself building. Then he scraped his teeth across her puckered skin and stars exploded behind her eyes as she fell.

Her entire body was lax, and she could only hear her heart beating rapidly in her head along with her labored breathing. Then she felt him shift over her and slowly slide into her.

"Kara," he whispered into her ear as he moved above her. "My god. You feel so good." He pulled back and looked down at her.

Reaching up, she tangled her fingers into his hair and pulled him back down to her lips. Pouring all of her feelings into this one kiss, she let it all go and held onto him as she gave him everything.

She must have fallen asleep shortly after her second release and didn't stir until Conner's alarm went off shortly after four in the morning.

"I thought you didn't have to work today?" She groaned.

He rolled over and shut the buzzing sound off. "They called me last night and asked if I'd fill in on some offshore training drills for Reagan, who is out sick." He sat up and rubbed his hands over his face.

She watched him, curious as to his morning rituals. Even though she was dog tired, she surmised that he wasn't going to kick her out because he had to leave. Rolling over, she watched him wobble to the bathroom and tried not to chuckle when she overheard him hit something and curse.

"You okay?" she asked.

His mumbled response caused her to smile. She rolled over and must have fallen asleep again. This time when she woke, Conner was sitting on the edge of the bed, looking down at her.

"What are your plans for the morning?" he asked, running his hand over her hip.

"Right now, I'm going to spend as much time as possible enjoying the quiet and this massive bed." She stretched her arms over her head, exposing her breasts since she was still naked under the blankets.

His hand moved up and cupped her breast and she smiled.

"Sorry," he mumbled. "It was there and... well." He grinned down at her. "Man, I wish I could crawl back in there with you and spend the entire day making love to you."

She felt her heart kick a beat as she moaned and arched into his hands.

"Call in sick," she said softly.

He sighed and dropped his hand as he looked at her face. "Can't. Promise me something?"

She tried not to pout as her skin cooled where his hands had just been. "What?" She figured that if he touched her or kissed her again, she'd promise him anything.

But his eyes grew more focused. "Don't walk home by

yourself." His hand went to her face and gently cupped her chin. "Promise me."

She nodded as she swallowed the lump in her throat at the intense look in his blue eyes.

"I can swing by during my lunch break and take you back home. If you want, we can grab some lunch together?"

That sounded really good, so she nodded again. He smiled and leaned down to kiss her thoroughly, melting her further to his mattress.

"You'll wait here?" he asked and, since she couldn't think any further, she nodded in agreement.

"Good, now go back to sleep." He kissed her again before getting up and leaving her there to dream about him.

The next time she woke, light was streaming in the bedroom window and her cell phone was ringing. Without looking at the screen, she answered the call.

"Hello?"

"Kara, where are you?" her sister asked, a little breathless.

Kara pried one of her eyes open and looked around. She knew where she was but just wanted to assure herself that last night hadn't been a dream.

"Conner's place. Why?"

"I'll be there in five minutes. There's been an accident," Robin said quickly.

Kara sat up and blinked her eyes a few times. "An... who?" She felt her heart drop at the thought of their parents injured.

"I don't know, but one of the Coast Guard helicopters that had been out on training drills went down in the water," Robin said, sounding a lot like she was running.

"Conner." Kara's mind went blank and she started hyperventilating. "Oh my god."

Her sister's voice broke through the haze of panic that had filled her mind.

"Get ready. I'm almost there. We're going to head down to the beach and wait with everyone else in town," her sister said before hanging up.

She threw on the first thing she found, then tossed on her snow boots and heavy jacket just as her sister knocked on the door.

Without thinking, she turned the handle lock as she stepped outside and followed her sister down the staircase.

She was sitting in the old truck before she realized that her sister had gotten the thing started. Her mind kept switching between the practical things in life like that to full-on panic mode about the possibility that Conner could be injured or worse.

When they parked at the beach entrance, she realized Robin was right—they weren't the only ones concerned about the downed helicopter.

"Any word?" Robin asked someone they stopped by.

Kara's eyes were glued to the gray haze over the massive body of water directly in front of them. Sure, the sunlight was bright behind them, but over the Pacific there was no sun, no clouds, only a misty gray fog swirling slowly around that caused her eyes to go a little unfocused.

She hadn't realized she was crying until her sister wrapped her arms around her shoulders. "I'm sure he'll be okay," she whispered.

"Oh god." A gasp escaped her as she covered her mouth and closed her eyes. "I just found him. I can't..." She shook her head and willed Conner to be okay.

"Hey," someone said, then gently took her shoulders. Through the mist in her eyes, she realized it was Allison Jordan. "Conner's on the phone for you."

Her heart leapt in her chest as she fumbled for the cell phone Allison was holding out for her.

"Hey." Just hearing Conner's voice had her closing her eyes and taking a deep cleansing breath. "I've been trying to call you to let you know—"

"I... left my cell phone in your apartment." She had been so concerned about him that she hadn't even grabbed her purse.

"Anyway, I'm okay. I wanted you to know. I wasn't on the Jayhawk that went down. I only had a minute, but... Well, I didn't want you to worry."

She swallowed hard and nodded, then opened her eyes and met his mother's worried eyes.

"Thanks, I... I'm here with your mom." She glanced over and saw the rest of his family. "Your entire family. We're here on the beach. We'll..." She shook her head. "We'll be here, waiting to hear about everyone else on the helicopter that went down."

"Okay," he said, and she heard a loud noise and then he mumbled something to someone else. "We're heading out to look for survivors. Stay close to my mother so you can get updates."

"Okay." She hugged the phone to her ear to hear the rest since the sound was getting louder.

"Kara?" he said.

"Yeah?" She held her breath, waiting for his next words.

"I'd really like you to stay at my place again tonight," he said, causing her to smile.

"Just try to kick me out," she countered before the noise on his end got too loud.

He yelled, "See you later," and hung up.

For the next seven hours, Kara, along with everyone else in Pride, waited on the foggy beach for any word on the four crewmen that had disappeared with the helicopter. Each hour, Conner checked in with his folks and made sure that they passed on an update to her and anyone else within earshot. She even had the chance to talk to him a couple other times. But she'd locked his front door on her way out, so she hadn't returned to his apartment.

Food from the Golden Oar was handed out to the crowd along with hot drinks. Chairs were even brought for the growing crowd.

It wasn't until after midnight that they had word that the downed helicopter had been found and all four of the crew were safe and sound. They'd been floating in a small inflatable raft, and some were injured and possibly had hypothermia. There was a large sigh of relief from the onlookers just before everyone dispersed.

Her sister drove her back to Conner's place and waited in the truck until he pulled into the parking lot. Just seeing him climb out of his truck still wearing his uniform set her heart skipping.

He gave her a slight grin, and she practically melted.

"Wow, he looks really hot in that uniform," her sister whispered.

"Ya think? Night," she said before climbing out of the truck and rushing to wrap her arms around him. God, he felt so wonderful that she didn't want to let go of him. But when her sister honked her horn as she pulled out of the parking lot, Conner took a step back.

"What do you say we head upstairs? I'm dying to get out of this uniform," he said with a smile which caused her heart to flutter as her insides did little jumps. Then he took her hand and led her up the stairs.

CHAPTER TWENTY

God, it felt good coming home to Kara after a long crazy day. He couldn't count how many days in the past few years that he'd spent a full day scanning the waters below. This was, however, the first when visibility had been almost zero. Everyone had been on guard and stressed. Not to mention that it was his own men down there in the cold water, some of whom he'd helped train for situations just like this.

Even now, as he led Kara back up the stairs to the apartment, his entire body was tense.

Shutting the door behind him, he didn't allow Kara to get a word out before pulling her into his arms and kissing her.

He couldn't help being a little out of control as he expressed exactly what he wanted, needed from her. His hands moved on their own, running over her hips, traveling lower until he hoisted her up and turned at the same time to pin her against the door. Their mouths never left one another as she tugged his leather jacket off his shoulders.

Her coat hit the ground shortly after his had, along with the rest of her clothes. Somehow, miraculously, he was still in his Coast Guard uniform of blue pants and dress shirt. Kara had removed his tie and had unbuttoned his shirt but hadn't pulled it off his shoulders as she ran her hands all over his chest.

He had to admit, he sort of lost it for a while. But when her nails scraped across his ribs, for just a moment he regained enough brain cells to remember to pull a condom out and slip it on before losing himself into her completely.

"My god, I don't think I can move," she said from her position tucked in his arms on the sofa, where he'd carried her after completely letting go.

"I didn't hurt you, did I?" he asked, feeling guilty about not being as gentle as he'd hoped.

Instead of answering him, she chuckled and rolled over until she looked into his eyes.

Her hand came up and she buried her fingers in his hair. "You can do that..."—she leaned over and kissed him slowly before purring—"to me anytime."

He smiled and wrapped his arms around her. "Yeah? So, I take it you like the uniform?"

She chuckled. "You may just have to put it back on and let me check again." She wiggled her eyebrows as her hands moved down his neck to his shoulders.

"Keep that up and we won't get much further than this sofa tonight," he warned.

"Good," she said against his lips.

"Yeah," he said after kissing her for a while. "But, unfortunately, I didn't have much of a lunch." His stomach growled loudly.

She frowned over at him. "I hadn't thought..." She shook her head and then suddenly rolled off the sofa and glanced around for something to wear. He watched her sexy bare ass as she moved towards the front door and bent over to pick up his uniform shirt. She slipped it on, and it hit her mid-thigh. He smiled when she buttoned up only a few buttons.

"I think that thing looks better on you than me." He sat up and watched her move into the kitchen. She smiled over at him.

"I'm going to make you something." She looked into his fridge, then frowned. "Gosh, is this all you have? A few eggs and half a loaf of bread with some cheese?"

"Yeah, I grabbed a few things last night but hadn't hit the fresh food section yet. I have a ton of frozen food, but usually hit the store for fresh items before eating." He started to pull on his pants again, but then instead grabbed all their discarded clothes and headed into the bedroom. Pulling on a pair of sweats, he returned to the kitchen to see Kara flipping French toast on the stove.

She glanced over at him and smiled and, for a split second, he completely lost his heart. Her long hair was messy, falling around her face. His eyes scanned over her sexy legs and ended on her red painted toenails, which were begging for attention. God. She was just... perfect.

Walking over, he wrapped his arms around her, gently moved her hair aside, and placed a kiss on the base of her neck.

"Mmm, maybe I'm not as hungry as I thought I was," he said against her skin as he felt himself growing harder.

"Oh no, after smelling this, now I'm the one who's starving." She giggled when he trailed a kiss to just behind her ear. He made a mental note about the ticklish spot and continued on to enjoy her earlobe.

His hands explored under the shirt that she'd put on as she continued to try and focus on making them breakfast for dinner.

He kept trying to distract her, but she kept chuckling and pulling away from him.

"Why don't you find us something to drink?" she asked, dodging his hands again.

He sighed and stepped away, only because his stomach had growled loudly again. Finding a bottle of sweet white wine and some orange juice, he decided to make mimosas since Kara was in a breakfast mood.

"How perfect," she said, taking the glass from him after setting a plate of French toast down on his kitchen table. The table had sat in his parents' house for years and had finally been replaced by a newer table. This one had been stored in the barn.

Actually, glancing around the apartment, everything that currently filled his new home had at one point filled his parents' home. He'd pretty much cleaned out the storage area in the barn when he'd moved in.

Taking his first bite, he sighed at how wonderful the simple food was.

"Wow," he groaned. "Why does your French toast taste so much better than what I make?"

She chuckled. "All food you don't make yourself tastes better." She motioned with her fork.

He thought about it and nodded. "I guess that's true." He shoveled more food into his mouth.

"It's really a good thing everything ended up okay today," she said after a sip of mimosa.

He set his fork down and took a moment to settle his thoughts before speaking. "It could have been so much worse. When we found the wreckage..." He shook his head and remembered seeing the chunks of metal floating in the dark water. "We all thought the worst."

Kara set her own fork down now and gave him her entire attention.

"Some of the new guys, well, they wanted to call off the search." He shook his head and frowned. "It took us two more hours to spot the orange raft and the men in it." He picked up his fork again and finished the rest of his meal. He had to admit, it felt wonderful having someone to talk to after a long day.

"I was so scared," she said, pushing her almost-empty plate away and looking over at him. Her eyes searched his, and he could see the concern flash there. He reached over and took her hand in his, tangling his fingers with hers. "Your entire family was afraid." She looked down at their joined fingers.

"Yeah," he said, feeling his heart sink. "I know. My unit was getting ready to head out when we heard the news of the crash."

Her eyes locked with his, then she surprised him by moving over and climbing onto his lap and kissing him. "I don't think I've ever been as afraid before in my life."

His arms tightened around her. "I know it's only been..."—he thought about it and laughed—"a few weeks," he admitted, "but how would you feel about moving in here with me?"

Her smile brightened and he relaxed. "I think I can handle that." She kissed him again. "Just as long as we do a little more food shopping."

He chuckled and kissed her again. "It's a deal."

That night, as he lay in bed with Kara wrapped around him again, he kept dreaming of the crash. But this time, instead of the wreckage from the helicopter, it was a small blue sailboat with a blue compass rose on its white sails.

The small boat was going down fast as he hovered overhead in the rescue helicopter, helplessly watching.

Conner called out to anyone below through the speaker system from his position working the winch. He was just prepared to signal that he was going to have to head down to search the water and the vessel when a man stepped out onto the deck of the small boat and looked up at him with a smile. Then he noticed the name painted on the hull of the boat. He continued to look down at the Dawn-Treader and his grandfather as they both disappeared into the dark ocean waters below.

Conner jolted awake, his heart racing and his mind foggy as to where he was and what had just happened.

"Conner?" Kara's hand came up to his shoulder as he sat up in bed. "Are you okay?"

After taking a few deep breaths, he laid back down and pulled her into his arms. "Yeah, just..."

"Bad dream?" she asked into his chest.

"Yeah," he agreed. "Sorry, I didn't mean to wake you." He kissed the top of her head and started tracing little circles on her bare shoulder.

"Want to talk about it?" she asked in a sleepy voice.

He thought about the dream again and sighed. "I watched my grandfather's boat going down." He shook his head. "It doesn't really make sense, but... I guess part of me wishes he'd had the Coast Guard there to save him. Growing up and hearing the story from my dad about the day we lost grandpa George and my dad lost his hearing, I've always wondered why no one had been there to save him."

She leaned up and looked at him as she rested her chin on her hand that was covering his chest. "Today's events mixed with your own past?" she asked softly.

"Yeah." He'd had enough sessions with the on-staff shrink to know that the job was hard and sometimes it messed with your mind. Especially after he'd pulled his first body out of the water. He sighed and pulled her down to kiss her. "Part of me has always wished I could have met the man. After all, he's the one who molded my dad, aunt, and uncle into who they are and, in turn, they have raised everyone in the Jordan clan." He smiled thinking of his large family.

Kara's smile brightened up the darkness of his mind, sending the rest of the dark thoughts retreating even further. He pulled her down and kissed her.

"I really am sorry I woke you." His hands ran up her back as she arched against him.

"Hm, I think I know of a way you can make it up to me," she purred as she rolled on top of him.

The following morning, as they were eating breakfast at Sara's Nook, Kara answered a call from her parents.

Every person he'd run into so far had congratulated him on a successful rescue. Becca even gave him a free coffee and donut, which he quickly scarfed down before enjoying his breakfast quiche.

He remembered as she was talking to her parents that they had dinner planned at his cousin's place later that evening. For a moment, he thought about trying to get out of the family get-together, but then he remembered the last time he'd tried to get out of a family dinner and knew he'd rather suffer through the evening than suffer through another year of hearing about missing the dinner.

"Okay, see you soon," Kara said before hanging up her phone.

"Your folks are coming?" he asked.

"Yeah. They wanted to look at the land and meet with

Rose and Jacob. I guess they've been talking to her about floor plans and options." She rolled her eyes. "Which I'm sure you've been thinking about yourself for your place."

He frowned. "No, actually, I haven't even thought about it yet."

She sighed. "Their visit shouldn't interfere with our dinner tonight. I'll have to stop by my place and grab a change of clothes."

"We can do that after breakfast. What time will they be here?"

"In about an hour. They were on the highway already."

"Maybe we can meet them up at the job site and then grab some lunch after?" he suggested. Her eyebrows slowly rose. "What?" he asked, curious about the look she was giving him, as if she was trying to figure him out.

She shook her head and then smiled. "Nothing, it's just..."

Suddenly, he could see a flash of nerves behind her eyes and realized that she was probably nervous about him meeting her parents.

Reaching across the table, he took her hand in his. "You do realize that I've met your parents before, right? I may not remember every detail of the meetings, but I'm pretty sure I've been around them my entire life."

"Oh?" Her eyebrows shot up and then she sighed. "Right."

He smiled. "I know you guys have been coming here forever, but this will be the first time with this." He held up their joined hands.

"Right." She smiled. "I don't think that will be an issue. My parents have worshiped all things Jordan for years."

He chuckled. "Good, then maybe they won't hate the idea of us living together."

She bit her bottom lip and winced slightly.

"Or not?" he said.

"Let's just leave that part out for now," she suggested. "It's not that they're old fashioned or anything, they just wouldn't want..." She sighed and then chuckled. "Never mind. It's better if we told them later."

He shrugged slightly. "They're your folks. You know them better than I do. But you will let Robin in on it?"

She laughed and nodded. "I've already talked to her about moving out."

"And?" he asked, feeling a little nervous.

"She was excited and happy for me. She claims she's going to turn my room into an office," she replied with a grin. "What about your parents?"

He chuckled. "Something tells me my mother is going to be thrilled. I actually think she was rooting for us before we even kissed."

Kara's smile doubled. "Yeah, I'd agree to that as well. I think the day she showed up on the beach to talk to me, she was already plotting out how to get us together."

He chuckled and lifted her hand to his lips. "I'm so glad it worked."

"Me too," she said before pulling out her phone and calling her parents back.

CHAPTER TWENTY-ONE

There was nothing more nerve-racking than watching your parents casually interact with the man who had spent all of last night completely pleasing you in bed. Especially when Conner couldn't stop touching her and sending her heart rate spiking.

Oh, she knew that her parents surmised that they were together. Of that there was no doubt less than five minutes after they'd met them at the construction trailer.

The doubt most likely fled their minds when Jacob blurted out that he was thankful Conner was at least taking a real date to the family dinner that night since he was stuck taking Rose.

Rose immediately slugged Jacob on the shoulder and scowled at him.

Rose then ushered her parents into her office, where they spent the next hour or so going over each floor plan and options.

Who knew there was so much that went into picking out a new home? Not only were there subtle changes in each floor plan, but then there were color options for the exterior of the home, including brick choices and window and door choices. Then there was the inside. Her mother seemed to be enjoying picking out flooring, cabinets, door handles, sink shapes, and the hardest choice yet, toilet bowl handles.

An hour and a half after her folks had stepped into the trailer, they walked out of it with Jacob to go stroll through the lots and finally decide which one they preferred. Kara was still rooting for her favorite lot at the base of the hill for them.

She was a little shocked when Conner asked her to stay behind to give her opinion on his own home choices.

Kara could tell that Rose was trying to act as casual as she could, but she noticed a spark in the woman's eyes that clearly showed she was wondering about their relationship.

Was this a subtle hint from Conner that he wanted things between them to move beyond living together? She hadn't even officially moved in yet.

Okay, facts first, she thought as Rose went over the many options with Conner.

Kara had technically known Conner most of her life. She had faint memories of playing with him and all of the other Jordan kids whenever they visited Pride during her childhood.

Had he ever stuck out in her mind? Maybe.

There had been one summer where she'd had a crush on him back in fifth grade. Though she was questioning whether it had been him or his brother Jacob at this point. In all honesty, she'd been crushing on all the Jordan boys, so she didn't blame herself for not remembering if it was Conner or Jacob that summer.

Next fact—her feelings for Conner were deep, even at this early point in the relationship. He wasn't like the other guys she'd dated over the years. She doubted he would cheat on her or decide one day that he no longer wanted to be with her. Well, at least she hoped.

They hadn't really discussed their relationship deeply yet, but he had told her how much he desired her. Just as much as she desired him, even now, as he frowned down at the many floor choices.

"What do you think?" Conner turned to her.

She walked over and looked down at the six different hardwood flooring choices. She knew which one she liked but wasn't sure it would go with all the other choices Conner had made so far.

"I like this one," she replied quickly. "But I'm not sure it goes with the cabinets you picked out."

He nodded. "Yeah, that's my favorite as well. I was thinking the same thing." He walked over to look at the cabinets again and held up the sample of flooring to the cabinet choices. "What do you think about these instead?" he asked, holding the chunk of wood up against soft gray cabinets.

"Those look good together."

Conner turned to her and smiled. "What are your thoughts about carpet colors?"

By the time her parents and Jacob walked back in the trailer, they had picked out every option for Conner's place.

"How did you come up with all these choices?" Conner asked Rose. "If memory serves me, you couldn't pick which bikini you were going to wear to the Fourth of July party when you were sixteen."

Jacob laughed and earned a glaring look from Rose.

"Blake," she answered quickly. "She's the one who narrowed down all these choices for us. She's pretty amazing. She's even agreed to decorate the model home when it's done," Rose added.

"She helped us out with decorating the barn for Sunset Wedding," Kara added. "She really is amazing."

"We haven't met Blake yet," her mother chimed in. We're looking forward to meeting her at the dinner tonight."

Kara's eyebrows shot up. "You... you're going to the dinner?"

Her mother chuckled. "It's one of the reasons we came down tonight. I had a really nice chat with Megan, who invited us along."

Kara had believed it was a Jordan family dinner only. There was no way she was going to keep the fact that she was planning on moving in with Conner a secret after tonight.

She figured that over lunch, she might as well rip that bandage off quickly.

Shortly after noon, the five of them, including her sister, walked into the Golden Oar and sat out on the back deck. The sun had come out and melted the snow and heated everything up nicely.

"I don't think I will ever get tired of this view," her mother said, leaning into her father's shoulder.

"With some of the snow still on the ground, it reminds me of our first time here," her father added with a slight grin.

Robin groaned slightly and rolled her eyes. Kara nudged her on the shoulder, and they settled back to hear the story they'd both heard a million times. Still, she loved to listen as her parents retold how they'd been snowed in one Christmas and had found themselves stuck in Pride, all for Conner's benefit.

There was more laughter and wine than any other lunch she'd had with her parents before.

"It's strange how one tiny decision can change the

course of your life," her father said, holding her mother's hand. "If I hadn't been roped into driving you home that Christmas"—he lifted her mother's hand to his lips, much like Conner had done to hers that morning over breakfast —"then we would've never explored our feelings for one another."

She looked over to Conner and realized the same was pretty much true for them. If he hadn't been out for a swim and she hadn't been almost drowning—it was past time to admit this to herself in her own head—then they wouldn't be here now.

"I'm moving in with Conner," she blurted out.

Instead of shock or concern flashing across her parents' faces, they both smiled at them as if they had already known this news.

"That's wonderful dear," her mother said easily.

Kara narrowed her eyes. "Something tells me you already knew?"

Her mother chuckled and glanced over at her father. "Another reason we were invited for dinner. Megan and I have been long-distance best friends for years." She shrugged. "She hinted at the news over the phone call."

Conner smiled over at her. "I should have warned you; my family can't really keep secrets."

When they were done enjoying their lunch, and just before clouds cooled things off outside, her parents claimed they were going to head to the B and B and get some rest before getting ready to go to Riley and Carter's for dinner.

"We've met both Carter and Corey on several occasions. They are such wonderful men and are so perfect for the girls," her mother said easily as they all walked out to the parking lot.

"Yeah, they fit in the Jordan clan perfectly," Conner added.

"And your cousin Suzie just married Robert and Amelia's son, Aiden?" her father asked.

"Yes." She smiled. "We held the wedding at the barn." She motioned between Robin and herself.

"We sure are proud of you girls," her mother added with a sigh. "Now, I'm in need of a nap. But maybe a walk on the beach first so all that wonderful food settles." She rubbed her flat stomach.

Kara watched her father take her mother's hand in his. Even now, twenty-five years later, anyone with eyes could see the love between her parents. It warmed the heart, and sometimes, according to Kara and Robin, who'd had to watch all the PDA between their parents their entire lives, could be a little too much.

Still, her entire life she'd dreamed of finding a man as dedicated to her as her father was to her mother.

After watching her parents and sister drive away, Conner turned to her.

"A walk on the beach sounds good. What do you say to a short walk, then stopping by your place to grab a few things before getting ready for dinner?"

"That sounds like a good idea." She took his hand, then followed him down a set of stairs to the side of the restaurant that led down towards the beach.

"So," he said after she reached down and removed her tennis shoes, leaving them at the base of the stairs with his. He'd rolled up his jeans slightly and she was thankful she'd pulled on a pair of capris earlier that morning after hearing the weather report. "I think that went well with your folks."

She smiled over at him. "Yeah, I should've known that they'd love you."

"Everyone loves me," he said with a silly grin.

She nudged his shoulder with her own as he took her hand and started walking down the wet sand.

"I hear we're supposed to get rain later tonight." He glanced off over the water and she followed his gaze. Sure enough, the skies were already dark in the distance.

"Snow, sunshine, rain." She shook her head. "Oregon weather."

He chuckled. "Still, when the sun comes out"—he lifted his face to the sun and sighed—"it makes it all worth it."

She did the same and sighed at the warmth on her face. "Yeah," she agreed. "It does. I still love rainy mornings though."

"You know, when I was younger and had to walk to the bus stop, while everyone else rushed to the stop or hid under umbrellas, I was the kid splashing in all the puddles and trying to catch raindrops on my tongue," Conner said with a smile.

"I used to go out in the yard with my umbrella during a rainstorm and hide under it like it was a large tent." She chuckled.

He stopped and pulled her into his arms, and she felt her heart skip.

"I'm thankful," he said, looking down into her eyes.

"For?" she asked, wrapping her arms around his shoulders.

"That I rescued you," he said with a slight smirk.

"Oh?" She cocked her head to the side. "I thought we both agreed that I didn't need rescuing."

He chuckled. "Think what you want, just as long as the outcome was the same. I pulled you from the water, and I'm not going to give you back anytime soon." He kissed her with a kiss that had her toes curling and her heart jumping out of her chest.

They continued to walk down the beach until his phone chimed, and he had to answer a call from his mother, who wanted to know if her parents had arrived safely.

Then they stopped by the cottage, and she packed a suitcase of her clothes and other items she would need for the next week.

She briefly talked to her sister about the coming week's schedule and assured Robin that she'd be back over there tomorrow morning for her meeting with the young couple to finish the arrangements for their wedding that following weekend.

She knew she could easily balance living with Conner and work. After all, the apartment was less than two blocks away from the venue.

Besides, just knowing that she would be spending each night wrapped in his arms was worth the extra steps she'd get each day. At this point in their relationship, she'd gladly walk miles for the pleasures he gave her.

She'd never lived with a man before and taking the big jump this time just felt right. After all, even if she hadn't admitted it to him yet, she'd never felt this much for a man before.

CHAPTER TWENTY-TWO

Being surrounded by your family always felt good. Even when they were all razzing you about the events of the last week. Being part of the group that rescued the downed crew, convincing Kara to move in with him, and purchasing a home all ranked top of the list in the family conversation.

That was until everyone sat down for dinner and Riley and Lilly both stood up and held up their water glasses.

His family was crowded around large dining table in the massive dining room since the rain had started shortly before they'd arrived. Normally, they'd all be out in the backyard gathered around the grill and playing tag football in the yard.

"We wanted to thank everyone," Lilly said, getting everyone's attention, "for coming out on such short notice."

"We especially wanted to thank all the extra guests who were able to make it tonight." Riley motioned to Kara's parents and to Rose, who was sitting as far away from Jacob as possible. "It's always great to have extended family share in special announcements."

A hush fell over the entire group. Conner swore that if

someone would have coughed, it would have broken the magic of the moment.

Riley glanced over at Lilly, who nodded at her cousin. Then they both turned to their husbands, who quickly stood up as matching grins filled the brother's faces.

"We're pregnant," Corey and Carter said at the same moment.

Several things happened at once. Every woman in the place sighed at the same time while every man in the place grinned from ear to ear.

For the next few moments, congratulations were passed around like hors d'oeuvres. Carter and Corey either had their hands shaken or were hugged and cried all over, depending on who was handing them out.

Conner walked over to his little sister and wrapped his arms around her, then kissed the top of her head. "Congratulations, squirt," he said, using her nickname. She pinched him in response. Chuckling, he shook Carter's hand. "So, I'm a little confused," he said loudly enough to get the attention of several other family members. "If Corey and Carter are the ones who are pregnant, why are you and Lilly the ones getting fatter?" He put a hand over his sister's flat belly.

The comment earned him an elbow in the gut from his sister and chuckles from the rest of his family.

Thankfully, this news caused all conversations about him and Kara to stop. They focused on when the babies would be arriving, sometime next spring. Lilly's due date was a full week before Riley's was, yet they dreamed of having their kids born on the same day. They hadn't determined the sex of either of their babies yet, as it was still too early. But they planned on having one big gender reveal party as soon as they knew.

For the rest of the evening, his mind turned to his own future and kids. In his mind, he continued to see images of children who looked an awful lot like a mix between himself and Kara.

He knew he'd moved fast in asking her to move in with him, but thankfully, she hadn't shied away from the challenge of being with him. It wasn't as if he was a difficult person to live with. Okay, so he was hardly ever around during the week and tended to forget about planning meals. But that's why it was such a great thing that he was living above a grocery store. He could stop off and get anything he wanted for dinner moments before stepping inside his home.

He knew that when they moved up to the home in Hidden Cove, things could change. He'd have to get good at planning meals and maybe even get one of those large freezers he could fill up for inside the garage.

Either way, having Kara's input meant a lot to him. After all, at this point, he imagined them living in the new home together.

Now all he had to do was convince Kara.

By the time they left his sister's place, he had pretty much talked himself into giving their relationship a couple months before asking Kara to permanently move in with him. By Christmas time, at least as he figured it, she'd be ready. Which meant he had the next few months to butter her up and show her just how great he was for her.

"What do you say to having lunch with me tomorrow?" he asked as they climbed the stairs. He held the umbrella above her head so she wouldn't get wet.

Even though they'd had the earlier conversation of enjoying the rain, he doubted she wanted to mess up her hair and outfit in the downpour that they were currently having.

"I'd say"—she turned to him just outside their door and wrapped her arms around his shoulders—"that it's a date." She kissed him.

"God," he sighed as her lips brushed against his. "I can't believe how wonderful you feel."

She smiled. "I'll feel even more wonderful once we get inside and you get these clothes off me," she practically purred against his lips.

He fumbled quickly to unlock the door as she chuckled beside him.

Once inside, it was all speed as clothes landed in piles on the floor trailing back to the bedroom.

When his shoulders hit the mattress, he smiled up at Kara, who had pushed him back and was now climbing on top of him as her hands moved to his chest.

"So, I was thinking," she said in a low sultry tone, "that I owe you."

"For?" he asked, crossing his arms behind his head as his eyes ran over the matching bra and panties she still wore.

"Smoothing things over..." she began as she reached for the clasp of her bra. Her words fell on deaf ears and his mouth went completely dry when she removed the last of the barriers, freeing herself to his gaze.

"Earth to Conner?" she asked, waving her hands in front of his face.

"Hm?" He shook his head to focus on her words.

Instead of giving her a chance to answer again, he leaned up and placed his mouth over one of her erect nipples, taking her fully into his mouth.

"God, I love the taste of you," he whispered, wanting

more. Shifting, he pinned her underneath him and continued moving his mouth over her heated skin. Each time he ran his tongue over a part of her, she tasted even better.

When his mouth ran into the silk of her panties, he licked the skin just under the hem, and she tangled her fingers in his hair.

"Don't stop," she begged him as he nudged the material aside.

"Nothing can stop me from pleasing you," he whispered against the newly exposed skin. When he ran his tongue across her sweet pussy lips, she arched and cried out, giving him exactly what he'd wanted. Proof that the last strings of her control were gone, just like his own.

The next morning when his alarm went off, Kara didn't even stir beside him. Trying hard not to wake her, he showered and dressed and was just stepping out of the bathroom when he realized she was no longer in bed.

Frowning, he stepped out of the bedroom to see her standing at the stove. Then the smell of bacon and coffee hit him, and he knew at that moment he was done for.

"What's all this?" he asked, coming up behind her and wrapping his arms around her.

She sighed and took the skillet off the stove.

"As I was trying to say last night"—she turned and wrapped her arms around him—"I owed you one for smoothing things over with my family. And," she said, giving him a quick kiss, "since you took over and..." Her face flushed slightly. "Well, you took over last night, so I figured the least I could do was make you breakfast."

He kissed her again. "You didn't have to do that. But since I smell bacon and coffee and you look so damn sexy wearing one of my shirts"—he pulled back to look down at the University of Oregon shirt she was wearing and her long sexy legs —"I'll take it."

"Good, because after, I'm heading back to bed." She kissed him again.

He chuckled as she filled two plates full of food for them and they moved over to the table together.

Sitting next to Kara eating breakfast and knowing that she was going to crawl back into their bed for a while longer had him wishing his days didn't start at five.

Even as he drove to the base, he was wishing he was back in bed with Kara. Then he walked in and saw the small celebration and the four crew members he'd helped pull from the water the day before and smiled.

Even though Ken had his arm in a cast and Reece had bruises and cuts on his face, the three guys and one woman, Reagan, were all smiles.

That high carried him through the rest of the day of training with the new recruits.

He was very surprised when he stepped into the apartment and was hit with a wall of delicious scents. Once again, Kara was standing at the stove, slathering butter on half of a loaf of bread. She glanced over at him when he walked in.

"Hey," he said with a smile when he noticed that the table was filled with candles and chilling wine. "What's all this?" he asked, walking over and kissing her on the back of the neck. She smelled better than the food she was cooking.

"I figured I still owed you a home-cooked meal to say thank you for helping out with the cottage." She leaned back into his arms.

"You made breakfast," he reminded her.

She chuckled. "Yeah, but that was toast, eggs, and bacon. Anyone can make that," she said with a shrug.

"Besides, there wasn't anything to eat here, so I decided to go shopping."

He walked over to the fridge and looked in. "Wow." He glanced over at her. "Was there anything left in the store when you were done?" he joked.

She chuckled. "I may have shopped hungry." She smiled at him. "Why don't you go get comfortable. This will be ready in a few minutes."

He walked over and kissed her again before heading in to shower and pull on a pair of sweats. He figured since she was wearing those gray leggings and another one of his T-shirts, he could go with comfortable attire.

When he came back out, she was pulling a pan of lasagna and the baked bread out of the oven.

"Just in time." She smiled over at him. "Why don't you pour us some wine. If you prefer, there's beer?" she added quickly.

"Wine is cool." He removed the wine from the cooler and poured them each a glass. Then he helped her bring the food to the table and even held out the chair for her. Instantly, he kicked himself for not stopping by his cousin's store and picking up a bundle of flowers. After all, this was their first official full day of living together.

Promising himself not to make the same mistake twice, he vowed to show Kara exactly how he felt about her and convince her that she was right where she belonged.

CHAPTER TWENTY-THREE

What was a girl to do? It seemed as if every time she turned around, Conner was making some grandiose romantic gesture. It had been almost four weeks since she'd officially moved in with him and, in that time, he'd returned home with flowers at least a dozen times.

He'd also woken up early on several occasions to sneak out and grab baked goods and coffee so that she wouldn't cook breakfast before he left for work, which had become a new norm she enjoyed each day.

He even spent his last two days off helping her and Robin around the barn for their events. She was feeling very pampered and didn't want it to stop any time soon.

She had never dated a man so doting before and was growing used to being spoiled. Even Robin pointed it out.

"Wow, you've got him wrapped around your finger," Robin whispered to her as they watched Conner empty the trash after Saturday's event.

Kara couldn't help but smile at that statement.

"He's being so attentive." She sighed. "It's..." She shook her head, unable to find the words.

"Exactly how Dad treats Mom," Robin added with her own sigh.

Kara hadn't really thought of it like that. Just hearing her sister say it warmed her even further.

"Do you think so?" she asked.

Robin nodded with a smile. "Everyone knows how the Jordan men are." Her sister tilted her head slightly and watched him bend over to pick up some discarded cups that someone had left on the floor. "Damn, not to mention how sexy all of them are."

"Hey." Kara nudged her sister. "Back off, that one's mine."

"Yeah, yeah," Robin waved her hand towards her. "I know. Still, too bad his brother..." Robin stopped talking when Conner moved closer.

"I think that's everything," he said to them.

"That's it then." Robin rubbed her hands together. "Thanks for the helping hand."

"Any time." He smiled as he wrapped his arms around Kara. "Ready to head home?"

Every single time he said those words, Kara's heart did a little flip.

"Yes." She smiled.

"Oh." Robin snapped her fingers. "I forgot to mention that the folks called. They've found a rental in Pride and will be moving down here at the end of next week until their new house is done."

"Oh?" She thought of how long her parents had been dreaming of moving to Pride. "That's wonderful."

"Yeah, your folks apparently found the place for them," Robin said to Conner.

"They did?" he asked with a frown. "Where?"

Robin shrugged. "It's on Clark Avenue. I guess it was on the land where your mother grew up?"

He smiled. "My grandmother's old lot." His smile slipped slightly. "The old house burned down a long time ago when my parents were just dating. My grandmother almost died in the fire, but my mom pulled her out just in time. Then shortly after my parents married and after my grandmother died, they had a new home built on the property and have been renting it out as an investment property ever since. I would have rented it out myself, but my folks told me they were having some things done in the place." He smiled.

"How wonderful," Kara said to him.

"It's just down about three blocks from our place."

"Are they going to sell their place?" Kara asked Robin.

"Sounds like they already have an offer on it," Robin added with a shrug.

"They've been waiting our entire lives to move here," she told Conner. "It's their dream come true."

He smiled down at her. "And by this time next year, we'll all be neighbors," he said easily.

She thought about his words for the rest of the night. Did that mean he wanted her to move into his new home with him? He hasn't asked her or for that matter even talked to her about it. Sure, he'd consulted her anytime Rose had had questions about his build. But as far as she knew, he just wanted her opinion.

His statement hadn't gone unnoticed by Robin either. The following morning, Kara received a text message from her sister.

"So, with what Conner said last night, does that mean he wants you to move into his new house with him?"

"I don't know. He's asked my opinion each time a question has come up about the house," Kara replied as she glanced at the closed bathroom door. All night long she'd dreamed about her future with him in the home overlooking the water.

What would it be like? Did she really believe he was the one for her? Her heart and mind kept screaming *yes*.

She had never been with anyone who was as attentive as Conner was. She figured she could easily get spoiled and had even gone out of her way the last time she'd been in Edgeview to stop by Victoria's Secret and had surprised him with a few sexy outfits, which he had thoroughly enjoyed.

The Jordan men had reputations around town as being completely devoted to the one they loved.

"Have you asked him?" Robin asked.

"No, I'm almost too nervous to do so," she admitted.

"Well, in a relationship, you have to be open and honest," Robin texted.

Kara thought about all the exes in her sister's closet and chuckled.

"Right, like you were with Matt? Or Carl? What about Tom?"

"Ouch, that stings. Go ask him. Take hints from my past mistakes."

Before she could respond, Robin texted her again. "Do you think he's going to ask you to marry him?"

Kara couldn't stop her heart from skipping at that thought. She'd been wondering that herself for a while now. Sure, they'd been dating for less than two months, but this was it. In her mind, Conner was the one, and she hoped that he felt the same about her.

"I don't know," she texted back, biting her bottom lip.

"Do you want him to ask you?" her sister asked.

"I haven't even thought about it yet, but… at this point I wouldn't say no."

"Eeeee!" her sister texted along with a little dance emoji. "So happy for you. I wish I could snag me a man."

"He's out there somewhere. Conner does have a big family…" she replied.

"I've met the rest of the Jordan men, remember. The only ones left are players. Besides, I'm far too busy right now to worry about men."

She felt guilty about spending her free time with Conner instead of being there to help Robin like she used to before Conner.

"I should be there helping you more," she texted back.

"Care Bear, go, talk to your man about how you feel. I've got this handled today. Love you. Bye."

Her sister's use of her old nickname made her smile.

"Thanks. Love you too."

When Kara walked out into the kitchen, she was surprised to see the kitchen table set and a beautiful breakfast laid out.

"What's all this?" she asked, walking over and placing a soft kiss on Conner's cheek.

"I had today off so I figured we could head up and watch them break ground on our new home." He wrapped his arms around her but must have felt her tense slightly at his words. "What?" He frowned down at her.

Titling her head, she looked up at him. "Nothing." She felt her heart skip at the lie but then he narrowed his eyes slightly and she knew she wasn't going to get away from talking to him. Sighing, she held onto him tighter. "You keep calling it our new home."

His frown grew. "I was hoping you'd get used to it." His eyes searched hers. "I was going to ask you over breakfast."

He motioned to the spread on the table. He dropped his hold on her, walked over, and pulled out the chair for her to sit.

Since he'd made it clear he'd planned it all, she figured she'd go along and moved over to sit down.

He sat down across from her and held up a glass of orange juice. She picked up her own and smiled.

"Kara." He smiled across the table at her. "I don't think it's a secret how I feel about you, but I realize that things are moving fairly quickly between us. But I can't imagine moving into the house without you. Please tell me you'll come with me."

She smiled. "Of course, I will." She lifted her glass to his and tapped it.

She had never spent a better day. Even the light freezing rain couldn't damper the joy she felt helping Conner push the shovel into the dirt and toss it aside and then standing there for almost half an hour as they watched a massive bulldozer clear the pathway where their home would soon be. Her parents' lot had already been cleared a few days earlier and there were men working on building forms where their foundation would go.

Once the rain started coming at them sideways, they climbed in their truck to watch the dozer work through the cold rain before heading out and meeting her parents for lunch at Baked.

After hearing from Robin last night that they were moving to Pride, Kara had called them and talked to them both. They were overjoyed at the possibility of finally living in their dream town.

Even though they weren't officially moving for a while, they had decided to start bringing some of their things down. Her father was retiring from his engineering position in Portland and her mother had already found a new job at the medical clinic just outside of Edgeview as a physical therapist.

Sitting in the crowded pizzeria across from her parents, she listened to them talk about how excited they were for the move.

"I start work at my new job Monday," her mother said with a smile. "The facility is state of the art. There is even an aquatic setup." Her mother practically squealed with delight.

She knew how much her mother loved her work and how much her father was looking forward to being retired. Seeing the thrill in both of her parents' eyes warmed her heart even further.

When she mentioned that they would neighbors soon and explained that Conner had asked her to move into the new home with him, they were both thrilled.

By the time they left the pizzeria, she was drained, and they spent the rest of their day snuggling on the sofa and watching movies as the rain turned into snow.

The following morning, she sent Conner off to work after a large home-cooked breakfast before heading to work herself.

Conner still didn't like that she walked to work each day, but since she enjoyed it, she convinced him that it was easier than driving the few blocks.

He'd even tried to convince her to purchase a small car for the short drive.

That morning, however, with the fresh snow on the ground and a thick chilly fog in the air, she had added an extra layer to stay warm.

Passing the flower shop, she waved at Suzie and Kate. The women were busy changing out the front window display in preparation for Halloween, which was only three weeks away. As a business owner, Kara knew that holidays tended to spread out and start early since customers were eager to get into the spirit.

She was just about to turn the corner when she heard tire squeals. She had a moment to tense just before some-thing hit her on the side of her head, just above her ear. Her left arm jerked forward as if it had been hit by an invisible force. The sting in both places didn't register until her body was flung towards the pavement. The echo of the gunshots registered the moment she hit the fresh snow, looking up into the dark grayness of the sky.

Her only thought, as the cold and grayness overtook her, was that she hadn't told Conner that she loved him yet.

CHAPTER TWENTY-FOUR

"Don't you dare die on me," Conner begged Kara as he looked down at the blood-soaked snow beneath her body. He was holding a clean rag against her temple. Or trying to, at any rate. His hands were shaking so bad that he worried he wasn't doing any good to stop the flow of blood coming from the wound.

Suzie had called him less than five minutes before, screaming that someone had shot Kara.

Conner had arrived at the scene at the same time that Aiden had. Aiden was focused on the blood coming from Kara's arm, while Conner could only focus on Kara's face.

Her lying on the corner of the street soaked in blood was the worst thing he'd ever seen. She was as pale as the snow surrounding her, the snow not soaked in red, at any rate.

"God damn it, where is that ambulance?" Aiden cursed. "We need more blankets," he said over his shoulder to Suzie and Kate.

It was then that Conner noticed that both of them were

only dressed in jeans and sweaters, which were all covered in blood.

"I'll run back and grab some more," Kate said, taking off quickly towards the store.

"We need to move her," Conner suggested.

"No." Aiden shook his head. "Not until we know if she's been hit anywhere else. We can't chance her losing more blood. She's already lost a lot."

It seemed to take the ambulance forever to get there. By then, they had covered her with a few more blankets to keep her warm. Aiden had tied a tourniquet around her upper arm and was yelling into his radio while he continued to hold the blood-soaked towel to her temple and spoke softly to her.

"Kara, sweetie, wake up. Open your eyes," he kept telling her over and over. But her translucent eyelids remained stubbornly closed.

He was pushed aside as the emergency medical crew started working on her.

Just as they were loading her into the back of the ambulance, Robin came running up the street. She hadn't even put on a coat or boots and was only wearing a sweater, jeans, and tennis shoes.

When she noticed the blood all over the snow and him, she cried out, and Conner had to catch her to stop her from running after the ambulance.

"Aiden's going to drive us to the hospital," he told her. "He can speed." He followed Aiden to the waiting cop car, pulling Robin along with him.

He didn't care that he was, himself, soaked in blood. Conner's eyes were glued to the back door of the ambulance, watching the shadows of the crew working on Kara in the back. He counted his heartbeats as the patrol car sped behind the ambulance.

Robin asked him questions, demanding answers, and he was thankful that Aiden answered them. It was impossible for Conner to even speak at this point. If anything happened to Kara, he doubted he would ever be able to put a sentence together again. His entire body ached; his heart felt like it was going to burst out of his chest.

Robin reached over and took his hand in hers, and he looked down at them. His hand, sticky with drying blood, and hers, pale and so much like Kara's that he felt tears sting his eyes.

"She's going to be okay," Robin kept saying.

He turned his eyes towards hers and noticed that she was crying as well.

Pulling her into his arms, he closed his eyes and sent up a silent prayer.

The three of them stormed the emergency room shortly after they wheeled Kara inside and disappeared through double doors.

"You guys wait here. I'll see if Aaron is around," Aiden said quickly.

Doctor Aaron Stevens, Conner's uncle, could be found some of the time at Edgeview hospital. Every surgery his uncle did was held at the newer facility they were now standing in.

"Who would do this?" Robin asked as they stood just inside the outer doors. "Why? Why shoot Kara?"

His mind snapped to what Suzie had told Aiden about seeing the blue truck speed away after they'd heard the shots and noticed Kara lying in the snow.

"It's all my fault," he whispered. "My family's." He closed his eyes and swayed slightly.

Robin's arm reached up to steady him.

"Aaron's not here," Aiden said as he approached them. "But Dr. Karen Logan is. She's a friend," he told Robin. "She's assured me that she's working on Kara now and will let us know as soon as she can."

Aiden motioned to the chairs. "We'd better sit down." His eyes ran over Conner, and he nodded towards a bathroom. "Why don't we go clean up first?"

Conner glanced down at his dark blue uniform and noticed the deep blood stains and the caked-on blood that covered his hands.

He followed Aiden to the men's restroom and scrubbed up as best he could.

When they stepped out, the small waiting room was filled with Kara's family and his own.

He was wrapped in his mother's arms, followed by his father's. Only then did he allow himself to lose it.

He felt even more arms wrap around them and heard others crying around him.

While they waited, speculation ran wild. Aiden was in constant contact as they hunted for the same blue truck that had sprayed them with dirt and rocks.

"It's got to be Thomas Carson's goons. I just can't figure out why they'd go after Kara," someone said.

"He came to the barn and talked to Kara a few months back. He said he was a lawyer and had an offer on our property," Robin said. "Then he stopped by and talked to me a few times." Her eyes moved to his. "I told him we weren't going to sell. He seemed to grow more agitated each time he stopped by. He kept claiming to be a lawyer and when I told him I knew who he was, he dropped the facade and offered me double what we paid for the property."

"What did you say to him?" someone asked.

"Why didn't you call me?" Aiden asked at the same time.

Robin avoided Aiden's question and instead answered the other.

"I told him that there was no amount of money that would make us sell," she said softly. "My god, do you think he did this to force me to sell?"

No one answered her until his uncle Todd jumped in. "That wouldn't make sense. The man is an egomaniac and a narcissist. I doubt he's a murderer."

"Still, it's worth looking into. If you see him around again, call me directly," Aiden said to Robin.

"Trust me, after this, I'm not going to let that man step foot on my property again," Robin replied.

What seemed like days later, a small dark-haired doctor walked out looking for them. He jumped up when he noticed her walking towards them.

"How is she?" several people asked as they all rushed the doctor.

The woman raised her hands. "She's resting," she said with a smile and looked around. "Where is the family?"

"Here." Kara's parents waved their hands. Robin was by their side as his family surrounded them.

The doctor turned to them. "Is it alright to share the update with the Jordan clan?"

Kara's parents nodded. "Yes, they're family," Alice said quickly.

"Kara was very lucky. The first bullet just grazed her temple, here." The doctor held up her hand to the spot on her temple that matched where he'd tried to stop the bleeding on Kara earlier. "This wound caused some bleeding even though it's only a mild abrasion. Head wounds tend to bleed more." She took a deep breath. "I've just come out of surgery for the penetrating gunshot wound on her arm. We've removed the bullet and stopped the bleeding. There appears to be some slight muscle damage. We won't know the full extent until after she wakes up. She should be able to make a full recovery after some physical therapy. But for now, she's in stable condition. They'll move her to her own room once she's out of recovery."

"Can we see her?" Alice asked.

"Not right now. Once they move her, she can have two visitors at a time."

His mind kept going over the fact that she was okay. That Kara was going to make it. That he'd be able to see her again. To hold her in his arms, to tell her that he loved her. Soon. He wanted to see her now.

"Doctor." He stepped forward after everyone started to go sit down again. "Is there any chance I could go back and see her now?"

The doctor ran her eyes over him. "Conner, you know what—"

"Please," he asked, his voice cracking slightly.

He'd known Doctor Karen Logan most of his life. Hell, the woman had not only set more than one of his broken bones, she'd been there for most of his childhood ailments, just as much as his uncle Aaron had been.

"You're involved with Kara?" she asked, her dark eyes running over him.

"I love her," he said clearly, which caused the doctor to smile.

"In that case." She glanced over to Kara's parents. "Is it okay if I take him back for just a moment?"

"Yes." Eric stepped forward with his arm still wrapped around his wife and daughter. Then he turned towards him.

"Tell her we're here and we'll see her soon," Kara's father said to him.

He nodded before following the doctor through the double doors.

He didn't know what he had been expecting, but seeing Kara hooked up to so many machines with tubes coming out of her nose, her mouth, and her arms, he almost broke down again.

She wasn't as pale as she'd been lying in the snow, and her hair was pushed away from her face as if someone had combed it aside. The blood that had covered her face had been washed away and a large white bandage covered most of her forehead.

Her left arm was wrapped tight and held up by a contraption above her body.

"Try not to disturb anything," the doctor told him. "I'll give you a few moments alone." She turned to talk to a nurse across the room.

He moved closer and ran his eyes over Kara. He knew she was in a drug-induced sleep and probably couldn't hear him, but he knelt beside her bed and took her right hand in his.

"I shouldn't have let you talk me out of buying you a car," he said softly. Then he leaned down and placed a soft kiss over her lips. "I love you. Come back to me." He felt a tear slip from his eyes. "I promise that I will spend the rest of my life making sure you are happy and giving you everything you could ever ask for."

He heard a sigh and knew that the doctor and nurse standing behind him had listened in.

"I love you," he said again before placing another soft kiss on Kara's lips.

CHAPTER TWENTY-FIVE

When Kara finally opened her eyes, she was so confused as to what had happened and where she was that it took almost half an hour for everything to register. Even then, she found it hard to focus and remember the details that her family had given her.

From the moment she opened her eyes, Conner was by her side. Even though he didn't say much to her, he was there, holding her hand. Of course, they hadn't been left alone since the moment she'd fought to get out of the drug-induced haze.

She didn't know what time it was or even if it was daytime or nighttime. The windows in her hospital room were covered and dark.

Every time she thought to ask, she would lose her train of thought. She fell back asleep to the sound of the machines working beside her and her family talking in hushed tones.

The next time she woke, the room was completely quiet and dark. She blinked a few times to make sure she wasn't just imagining the darkness. Seeing a few flashing lights and the bright exit sign over the door, she relaxed back and thought of falling asleep again when she heard someone shuffle beside her and glanced over to see Conner stretched out in a chair, his arms crossed over his chest. His head was at an angle, resting on the corner of the chair as if he'd fallen asleep in the oddest position possible.

She could tell instantly that it couldn't be comfortable.

"Conner?" she said after she'd cleared her throat. It felt raw, as if she'd been to a concert the night before and had screamed and sang until her vocal cords were abused.

He sprung up and rushed to her side.

"Are you hurting?" he asked her, taking her right hand in his.

She hadn't thought about it. Honestly, she'd been numb until he'd asked the question. After quickly assessing her entire body, she shook her head and winced.

"No," she said, mentally kicking herself for moving fast. "I'm okay. You shouldn't be sleeping there." She glanced over to the chair he'd been sitting in.

"I drew the short straw and got to stay with you tonight," he joked as he leaned on the edge of her bed.

"You can go home, get some rest," she offered.

His smile slipped. "I'm not leaving your side. Don't ask me to," he added softly. Then he lifted her right hand up to his lips. "How are you feeling?"

"Tired and hungry."

"I can see about getting you something to eat?" he offered.

"That would be okay," she said with a sigh. "What time is it?"

He pulled out his phone and glanced at it. "It's a quarter to one."

She blinked a few times. "In the morning?"

"Yes. Do you remember what happened?"

She thought back to what her family had told her the last time she'd been awake.

"I was shot," she said, still having a difficult time letting that sink in. "Do we know who?"

"Not yet. There is a statewide manhunt for the blue truck. Suzie's new cameras at the store caught the truck's plates. It is registered to a Kurt Collins. The man has several outstanding warrants."

She ran the name over in her head, trying to remember if she'd heard it before.

"Robin has assured us that you don't know any Kurt Collins," he said, as if reading her mind.

She relaxed slightly. "Now what?" She felt her head growing groggy again.

He leaned closer and placed a kiss on her lips. "Now, you get better and I take you home. Then, the first day you feel up to it, we go car shopping."

She smiled. "Sounds good so far."

He kissed her again. "Then we take that new car, drive into the city, and buy an engagement ring, the kind of ring you've always dreamed of." He kissed her slowly. "And when we're done with that, we plan our dream wedding."

She was smiling at this point. "And after that?"

He chuckled. "Well, then you'll be Mrs. Kara..."

"Marie," she supplied her middle name.

He nodded with a grin. "Mrs. Kara Marie Jordan. We'll move into our dream home." He kissed her again. "And have..." He frowned. "How many kids do you want?"

She thought about it. "Three."

He tilted his head slightly. "I can deal with three." He nodded. "Just as long as you like just as many dogs."

She laughed and then winced. "I love dogs."

"Okay, then we get started on our family. And live happily ever after."

"Oh?" She shifted slightly, this time realizing it hadn't hurt as much.

"Of course, this fantasy world is all contingent on you getting better," he warned. "We can't start our perfect life until you get some rest."

"And food," she reminded him.

"Right." He leaned over and hit the button on the side of the bed. When the nurse's voice came over the speaker, he asked for something to eat for her. "There. With food on the way, is there anything else I can do for you?"

She smiled and let out a relaxed sigh. "Tell me that you love me."

His smile grew. "I do," he said. "I love you." He kissed her again.

"I love you," she replied. "I want to have the happy life you've described. I want it all."

IT TOOK an entire week before she was finally released from the hospital. The days dragged on.

She was sore and didn't like to move her arm much. Her head didn't hurt as bad as her arm did and, within a few days, she'd removed the large bandage, which blocked some of her vision, and replaced it with a smaller bandage.

Conner had tried to entertain her by reading to her or watching movies with her. He had barely left her side. He'd only left her to go into work twice and had taken the rest of the days off.

Her family visited her as often as they could, even

though she knew they were in the middle of moving into the rental home in Pride.

Robin kept her filled in on their work and had said that Emma Auston, a recent high school graduate, had filled in for her while she was out. Robin had hinted that they could afford to keep the girl on even after Kara returned to work.

She had also been visited by every member of the Jordan clan. Each family had brought her flowers or gifts, wishing her a speedy recover.

Her mother, it was determined, would be her physical therapist once she was released from the hospital. She hadn't moved her left arm a lot since waking up.

Her mother kept trying to get her to move her fingers and each time she'd asked her to do something, she was easily able to obey.

As they drove home in the new snow, Conner filled her in on the progress of their new home.

"They're pouring the foundation as soon as the snow stops," he told her. "The framing should only take a day or two."

"That fast?" she asked, resting her head back. It had been almost a full week since she'd been outside in such bright lights, and her head was beginning to ache. She was also so exhausted from taking her first shower and getting dressed all by herself that she thought she could sleep for days.

"Yeah, framing is the fastest part. I thought we'd swing by there and have a look tomorrow."

"That would be nice." She stifled a yawn.

"You need to rest," he warned.

They parked in their spot in front of their apartment, and he surprised her by lifting her into his arms and carrying her up the stairs.

He set her gently on the sofa, and she felt relieved to be home. To be there, with him, knowing that they had so much to do in their future.

"We have enough frozen meals to last us two months. I think everyone in Pride delivered something for us to eat." He sat down beside her. "So, we won't have to worry about cooking." He wrapped his arm around her. "We even have half a dozen pies in the freezer," he added with a smile.

"That sounds... wonderful." She thought about the prospects of not needing to cook for a while.

"How are you feeling?" he asked.

"Tired." She rested her head on his chest. "And relieved to be home."

"There is one more thing I forgot to mention." He chuckled when she groaned.

"I think I'm done with surprises." She sighed and rested back.

"This one is a good one. I'll be right back." He got up and disappeared into the bedroom.

She tucked her legs up on the sofa and pulled the blanket over herself while she watched the snow falling outside.

She had just closed her eyes and felt herself drifting off when something cold touched her face.

Jumping slightly, she opened her eyes and laughed when a small black puppy licked her face.

Conner was holding the little thing over her, laughing.

"His name is Ralph," he said with a grin.

"That is a terrible name." She laughed and took the small thing from him, careful to only use her right arm since her left one was tucked against her body in a cast. The puppy nibbled on her chin, making her laugh.

"Carrie and Josh claims it's because he has a knack for

barfing up everything he eats." Conner laughed and sat beside her, getting the puppy's attention.

"How about you leave the naming to me?" She looked into the puppy's dark eyes. The little thing wiggled out of her hold and moved over to Conner. She watched the two play for a moment. When Conner stood up and moved over to put one of the meals someone from town had cooked for them into the oven, the little dog followed him around as if eager to see what he was doing and where he was going.

When Conner sat back down, she smiled as a name came to her.

"Shadow," she said clearly, causing Conner's eyebrows to shoot up.

"Hm?" he asked as he helped the small dog up on to the sofa.

"His name is Shadow. Because he follows you around everywhere." She chuckled when the puppy climbed onto her lap and quickly fell asleep.

Conner smiled. "I like it much better than Ralph," he admitted, leaning over and kissing her. "Now that we have the first new member of our family..." He kissed her again, but just then his cell phone rang. He let out a large sigh before answering it.

She half listened to his side of the conversation and focused even more when his eyes met hers and he frowned over at her. He hung up after only saying a few words.

"Who was that?" she asked.

"Aiden." He tucked his phone back into his jeans. "They've found Kurt Collins."

"That's good news." She felt much better knowing the man who had shot her was off the streets. "Where did they find him?" she asked.

"Just on the other side of the California state line." He stood up to look out the window.

"Good. He'll go to jail then?" she asked.

Conner shook his head and looked back at her. "No, he's dead. It appears that drove his blue truck off a cliff along Highway One. We won't be able to get answers from him now. We may never know if Thomas Carson hired him to shoot you or not."

She watched the frustration on his face grow to anger.

"Conner." She waved him towards her. When he sat back down beside her, she took his hand in her good one. "It no longer matters. I'm here, safe and sound. The police have extra patrols around town and the next time Thomas Carson steps foot in Pride, he'll have an escort right back out of town."

Conner sighed and nodded. "Yeah, you're right. I had just hoped that we could actually tie this to the man so we could lock him up."

"Let's not spend my first night home thinking about him." She shifted the small dog in her lap.

"Right," Conner reached over and stroked his finger down the small dog's nose. "You're home. Safe and sound. That's all that matters."

"And you love me," she added, earning a large smile from him.

"Right, and I love you," he said before kissing her.

Holding Haley

Missy's Moment

Breaking Travis

Roping Ryan

Wild Bride

Corey's Catch

Tessa's Turn

Saving Trace

The Grayton Series

Last Resort

Someday Beach

Rip Current

In Too Deep

Swept Away

High Tide

Lucky Series

Unlucky In Love

Sweet Resolve

Best of Luck

A Little Luck

Christmas Wish

Silver Cove Series

Silver Lining

French Kiss

Happy Accident

Hidden Charm

A Silver Cove Christmas

Sweet Surrender

Entangled Series – Paranormal Romance

The Awakening

The Beckoning

The Ascension

The Presence

The Calling

Haven, Montana Series

Closer to You

Never Let Go

Holding On

Coming Home

Pride Oregon Series

A Dash of Love

My Kind of Love

Season of Love

Tis the Season

Dare to Love

Where I Belong

Because of Love

A Thing Called Love

First Comes Love

Someone to Love

Wildflowers Series

Summer Nights

Summer Heat

Summer Secrets

Summer Fling

Summer's End

Summer's Wish

Distracted Series

Wake Me

Tame Me

Stand Alone Books

Twisted Rock

Hope Harbor

Raven Falls

For a complete list of books:

http://JillSanders.com

ABOUT THE AUTHOR

Jill Sanders is a New York Times, USA Today, and international bestselling author of Sweet Contemporary Romance, Romantic Suspense, Western Romance, and Paranormal Romance novels. With over 70 books in eleven series, translations into several different languages, and audiobooks there's plenty to choose from. Look for Jill's bestselling stories wherever romance books are sold or visit her at jillsanders.com

Jill comes from a large family with six siblings, including an identical twin. She was raised in the Pacific Northwest and later relocated to Colorado for college and a successful IT career before discovering her talent for writing sweet and sexy page-turners. After Colorado, she decided to move south, living in Texas and now making her home along the Emerald Coast of Florida. You will find that the settings of several of her series are inspired by her time spent living in these areas. She has two sons and off-set the testosterone in her house by adopting three furry little ladies that provide her company while she's locked in her writing cave. She enjoys heading to the beach, hiking, swimming, wine-tasting, and pickleball with her husband, and of course writing. If you have read any of her books, you may also notice that there is a love of food, especially sweets! She has been blamed for a few added pounds by her assistant, editor, and fans... donuts or pie anyone?

facebook.com/JillSandersBooks

twitter.com/JillMSanders

bookbub.com/authors/jill-sanders